Waltz of the Goblins

Melissa Matos

Momtoast Publishing

Waltz of the Goblins

Copyright © 2021 by Melissa Matos

For permission requests, please contact Melissa Matos at melissa@momtoast.com

ISBN
Paperback: 978-1-7364970-2-9
eBook: 978-1-7364970-3-6

Cover Design by Melissa Matos
Edited by Sarah "Sare" LaChance

melissamatosauthor.com

To my mom and grandmom,
who put up with a moody, geeky writer
trying to get through another book.

Chapter One

I came to my senses on the border between civilization and the Wild. My stomach ached. Well, everything ached, and I smelled of mud and fouler things. I had enough of my wits to crawl behind a tree, out of sight of the path beyond the edge of the forest and listen for the next Warden patrol to pass. The only sound around me was the forest, sleepy in the heat of a summer afternoon. I waited over an hour, hoping they wouldn't be long, knowing I would doze off again. Finally, three Wardens strolled by, heading west. Another patrol should pass in two hours. That gave me plenty of time to find the pack I had buried and make myself presentable.

Two weeks ago, I had buried my things under an old oak surrounded by skinny trees, and then gave myself over to the Wild. It took almost an hour to find the spot again. I usually woke close to where I had entered, but never in the exact spot. I rested again before digging it up. It was my usual Midsummer survival pack: a clean set of clothes, some food, and my illusion powders. I devoured nuts and cheese while I wandered to a stream that gurgled nearby. As I washed up, a few nymphs floated past, drifting lazily in the current, their hair splayed out like sea grass. At any other time I would have feared they would start a game at my expense, but after Midsummer every Wild thing was as worn out as I was, and not in the mood for tricks. Not even with a half-blood Changeling like me. Once I felt less disgusting, I changed clothes and got to work on my illusion.

If had emerged from the forest as my real self, with glowing amber skin and glimmering green eyes, the Wardens would kill me on sight. It was their job to make sure the Wild stayed in the Wild. But I couldn't don my usual face either—the one everyone knew as Glade Balladeer. She was rumored to be visiting her frail old mother back in Guowtan. Instead, I recreated the look I had worn just before losing myself in the woods. My hair grew long and blond, my skin lightened to a creamy shade of pink, and freckles dotted across my nose for good measure. I kept the dirty, worn look. If the Wardens out on patrol today couldn't take pity on that face, then they didn't have hearts.

The next patrol came by shortly. This one included someone in a good enough mood to be singing. They were following the footpath just outside the woods. It was not an official road, but something worn into the grass from years of Wardens keeping guard. So far, the Wild had kept its side of the bargain and not grown out over the border, so although there was no fence or wall, there was an distinct end to the forest all around Drakir.

I waited until they came into view and then threw myself out of the forest, shouting at the top of my voice, and half-stumbled, half-ran in their direction. I didn't have to put much effort into falling faint in their path.

"What's that?"

"Is she all right?"

"Careful!"

As the four of them gathered around me, their voices muddled together.

One grumbling voice rose above the others. "I said careful, she's probably some Wild thing!"

"She's not Wild," another argued. "Look, she's got a Warden's badge."

That was another wise touch on my part, making sure my Warden badge was prominent on my belt. That was no illusion either; I was an official Warden, licensed and registered, just like them. A woman crouched beside me, lifted my head and started checking me over for wounds. I blinked my eyes open and gasped, and she smiled down at me.

"It's all right, you're out now. What's your name?"

"Amalia," I answered. I had always liked that name. I struggled to sit up, but she held me firm. "I have to get away."

"You're safe now, just rest. Stop scowling, Ricard, and give us a potion. She must be the Warden that went missing from the South Tower two weeks ago."

Ricard, a dark-haired human with a sour expression, came into view over the woman's shoulder and handed her a small glass vial.

"Seems like she should be a mite worse off for being in the Wild a full two weeks," he said.

She huffed. "She's bad off enough." The woman pressed the bottle to my lips and made me drink. She didn't let me sit up until she had checked me over again. "Shaky and wobbly all over. You haven't eaten in a good bit, have you?"

"I couldn't very well eat while I was in there," I said, glad I had thought to rinse my mouth after munching my cheese. She helped me to my feet, and I got a look at the others, two red-haired dwarves who looked enough alike that I guessed they were siblings.

"Good girl," the woman answered. "Well, I'm Danny, and these two are Riln and Rian. And you've met Ricard. We'll get you back to the South Tower and fix you right up."

"Thank you, thank you so much."

The journey to the South Tower wasn't a long one, but I was weak from my time in the Wild and slowed the group considerably. I kept tripping over my own feet and falling behind. Danny would stop the group, and Ricard would complain that we would miss supper if we didn't keep moving.

Rian eventually began singing again. She had a strong, deep voice. I knew little about dwarvish music. It always sounded jarring and unresolved to me, but her singing made it sound hearty. At least it drowned out Ricard's complaining.

We arrived at the South Tower just as dusk fell. Warden towers were simple structures, tall and round with thin slits for windows. Wide panes of glass encased the top level, protecting an enormous pile of wood, so if a signal were lit, the neighboring towers would see and send help. Several floors inside housed supplies and sleeping quarters for the Wardens.

We were welcomed in, and space was cleared for us at one of the long tables on the first floor. The supper bowls were refilled, and we began passing them around and spooning large helpings onto the plates set out for us.

"You made it back, and without a mark on you," an older elf said, stopping by our table. I had stayed at the tower a few days before disappearing into the Wild, and this was one of the Wardens I had made a point of talking to. It was one of many steps I took to ensure no one discovered why I really disappeared every year. I couldn't remember his name, only that he was an elf and a fighter, with a notable scar on his chin.

"Yes, thank the Flames," I said.

"So what lured you in? You didn't go chasing a satyr, did you?" He nudged Ricard, who grunted and rolled his eyes.

"Of course not." I made a face and the others laughed. "I'm not that new."

"Get dazzled by the lights then?" Riln asked around a mouthful of food.

"No." I lowered my face and made myself blush. "It was flowers." They laughed at me again and I shrugged. "Poppies, I think. They were so beautiful, and I remembered if you can get the Wild ones, they are good for so many things. I thought I could just grab a few and get out."

That sobered them some. It would not be the first time a new Warden was lured into the Wild, but few of those stories ended as well as mine.

"As soon as I stepped in among the poppies, I fell asleep," I continued. "When I woke I was in a different part of the forest and had to find my way back."

"Just be thankful it was Midsummer and all the Wild creatures were somewhere else," Danny said, patting my shoulder. "Now eat up. Once you get a good night's sleep, you'll feel worlds better."

#

It felt so good to spend a night in a bed, with a fire in the room and walls surrounding me, even if I had to suffer through the nightmares. Faint memories of whatever I had been doing in the last two weeks always haunted me just after Midsummer. I was glad I never fully remembered what it was. The weariness and the filth afterward were enough.

I woke in the morning feeling well-rested and refreshed. I emerged from the stairs into the main foyer, which was crowded with Wardens exchanging reports with the night shift just coming in from patrol. Still hungry as a new kitten, I pushed through them to the dining hall. Breakfast was busy. Long tables laden with food and pitchers, and rough wooden chairs laden with Wardens filled the hall. I found an out-of-the-way table so I could gulp down some eggs without interfering with their business. They all assumed I had survived an ordeal in the Wild, so they considered me off duty, ready to head home as soon as I was strong enough to travel.

While I watched them bustle around, I felt a familiar humming, something that buzzed like fat and lazy summer flies. I hadn't felt it in a while, but I could think of only one reason it would show up now.

I hoped to make it outside before they found me, but as I stood up, I saw a brown-skinned human with an array of wands strung at his belt, and a short, round woman, her fair hair wound up in ornate braids. They hovered in the doorway searching the faces of the Wardens gathered for breakfast. They glanced right over me. I didn't look like myself, like the Glade they knew. I waved to get their attention, and they wove through the crowd to my table.

"Glade?" Otsoa asked when they reached me. Josie peered at me, a deep frown on her face. She was my best friend, and knew me better than anyone, but even she couldn't tell it was me beneath my disguise.

"It's Amalia for now," I said. "Had you fooled, didn't I?"

Otsoa didn't return my plucky grin. "All right, Amalia. We've come to take you home."

"Otsoa, is that you?" Ricard swung by our table on his way to meet his party. He seemed much more cheerful this morning. Maybe he had been missing some sleep as well. "Haven't seen you in a while. You were the only Warden that was at the towers more than Danny and me. And who's this?"

"Hello, Ricard, this is Josie. Sweetheart, this is Ricard. He's a bit gruff, but a good fighter to have in a scrap."

Josie smiled shyly up at Ricard. I wondered if Otsoa had introduced her as sweetheart before.

"Pleased to meet you," Ricard said.

"Lovely reason to be home more," Danny commented. She had come up behind Ricard and nudged him. "When do we get to settle down?"

"When you stop your heart from bleeding for every wounded traveler we find out there." Ricard shook his head. "Woman keeps me traipsing around Drakir like we're the flaming healer brigade. I'd like a few quiet months, yah know?"

"Sure, and after two weeks you'd be so antsy for a fight, you'd be starting brawls at the bar. Come on, let's get some breakfast before we're due out again." Danny dragged Ricard toward the buffet.

"You haven't been avoiding tower duty, have you?" I asked Otsoa.

"No, just haven't been going out as much. I was practically living in the towers before," he admitted. "Most towns didn't want to admit a non-licensed wizard."

"But you're licensed now," Josie said, slipping her arm under his.

"Yes, and you have that nice comfy inn. You ever sleep in a tower bed?" They chuckled together, and I turned my face down to my meal. Part of me was so happy for Josie; she deserved this. Part of me dreaded being the third wheel all the way back to Casavera, where Josie's inn was, and where Otsoa was now staying. It was only a few hours north from there to Cyfar, the city I considered home.

"So what happened?" Otsoa asked me, his voice growing serious.

I cringed. "Can we talk about it on the way back?" I looked around at the Wardens to see if any had overheard.

"Right." Otsoa's voice was clipped. Josie sighed and took a seat across from me at the table.

A few other Wardens stopped by to see how I was doing. I drank three more cups of coffee and had two heaping plates of food before I felt well enough to head out. As good as the night's sleep had been, I couldn't completely relax. That would mean losing the illusion I was wearing. It always took a little more concentration than usual to keep it going when it wasn't my natural face. I just needed to get home and back to my old self.

I walked out with Otsoa and Josie and found a large, ornate coach waiting for us by the doors. Josie's family crest was painted on the side: three white balls floating over a simplified picture of an erupting volcano. Four shining black horses in white harnesses were pulling the massive thing. The driver was in full livery, and it smelled like new leather inside.

"Why haven't we always traveled like this?" I asked.

Josie rolled her eyes and looked away. "My family gave me charge of a second inn, so I have access to this so I can keep tabs on it. You're just lucky no one else needed it today." I wasn't sure if she was upset with me or with her family.

"That's great, Josie. Sounds like you're doing really well. Must keep you pretty busy though."

"What happened, Glade? Where have you been?" Otsoa asked, his voice like a bucket of ice water down my back. I looked from him and back to Josie, who wouldn't meet my eyes, then looked down at the floor.

"I don't remember."

Otsoa groaned and sat back, exasperated.

Josie crossed her arms and turned to stare at me. "You don't have to keep things from us anymore. Just tell us what happened."

I tried to hide how much her words stung. It wasn't as though she was the only person I had kept my true nature from. I hadn't told anyone. Then I had lost control at her inn, and they had both found out.

"I'm not keeping things from you," I mumbled. "I really don't remember. I never remember." I blinked my eyes tightly a few times to be sure they wouldn't look misty when I looked up again. "I thought I explained this to you guys."

6

"You were gone for two weeks," Josie said. She pushed forward on the seat so she was looking up into my face. "Two weeks. Without a word. And Otsoa —"

Otsoa put his hand on her arm and she stopped.

"What's wrong? What happened to you?" I asked.

Otsoa took a deep breath and shrugged. "I felt it. All of it. And it made things . . . difficult." He pointed to the necklace he was wearing. It looked out of place with his otherwise rough clothing, a delicate silver necklace pendant shaped like a sword. A rose formed from a garnet hung from the tip. "I think we need to figure out exactly what this does."

"Did anyone get hurt?" I asked quietly. They shook their heads. That was something, at least. "It made you want to change?" I swallowed hard. Being born Wild as I was had many downsides. Getting a good job was impossible, and most people considered me bad luck to have around, but Otsoa had learned Wild human magic. He could turn into a jaguar, or rather, turn into a jaguar if he became too agitated. If they caught him using this magic again, he'd have more than his license revoked.

"I did change, twice," he said. "Both times at night, thankfully. Josie managed to keep me hidden."

"I'm sorry. I didn't know." It was a weak excuse, but it was all I could think to say. The necklace connected us. I could feel when he was near, and if he was trying to change into a jaguar, it would make me incredibly queasy. It was easy for him to change, but not so easy to come back. Somehow this necklace, gifted to us by a very strong Wild One, let me help him return to human form. I hadn't known it would work the other way and drag him into being a jaguar if I was Wild.

"We weren't prepared for it," Josie said. "Is this going to happen again?"

"Every Midsummer," I said. "Every time. If the Queen calls, I have to go. Most times of the year she doesn't know I exist. But in Midsummer she calls us all." I shrugged. "I don't have a choice."

"And you don't remember anything?" Otsoa asked again.

"Just bits and pieces. Flashes of images and feelings." I bit my lower lip. "Why, what do you remember?"

"Nothing much, just how it felt." He shifted in his seat. "Is it always like that? So . . ."

"Exhilarating?" I said. "Intoxicating?" I had thought he would look away, but he met my gaze with his large brown eyes. He felt sorry for me. I just nodded and looked away again.

It was an awkward ride. I knew they had more questions, but I didn't have any answers. They had tasted what the Wild felt like, Otsoa during Midsummer and Josie at her inn when I had lost control, but I was sure they didn't understand all of what I was up against. It was one thing to desire something, and quite another to be ruled by it.

Chapter Two

What few memories I had of the past two weeks involved open sky and the smell of damp earth and sunlight on my skin. Driving through the narrow stone lanes of Casavera, lined with iron fences and manicured trees, made me feel caged in. The coach turned into a small plaza surrounded by quaint shops with an enormous fountain bubbling at the center. Josie's inn, the Fonte, stood out, a blocky stone structure among the delicate elven buildings. I breathed easier when we stopped into the cool dim foyer. At least this felt like home.

I followed Josie into the dining room and found my half-brother pacing around like a caged animal. As soon as he saw me, even though I was still wearing Amalia's face, he rushed over and grabbed me by the shoulders.

"Where is she?" he pleaded, his gray eyes wide with fear.

"Where is who?" I asked, trying to pull out of his grip. His fingertips were digging into my shoulders. "It's me, Glade. I just need to change my face—"

"No," he growled shaking his head and me at the same time. "I know it's you. Where's Ura?"

"Oh." He didn't care that I was back. I suppressed a sob. "Oh Glenn, I'm so sorry."

"Where is she? Did she come back? Did you see her at all?"

"I don't know. I might have seen her, but I wouldn't remember."

He pushed me away, disgusted, the same expression on his face as Josie had in the coach. "She hasn't done this in two years, and then you show up again and now she's gone." He started pacing again.

His words stabbed, though there was no way this was my fault. Changelings could be born of all kinds of Wild folk, and Ura was part sylph. Sylphs, even part ones, were notoriously flighty and disappeared on a breeze, sometimes literally. Being half Nepaea, a nymph of the valleys, I was more grounded and likely to return to a place I was attached to. It was a miracle Ura had cared enough about Glenn to stick around for two years. I had never stayed through Midsummer.

"I'm sorry," I mumbled.

"Sorry won't bring her back." His voice was hoarse, and when he swung around to stare at me, I noticed red around his eyes. I had never seen Glenn this unsettled, not even when we'd been battling wizards and Wild creatures both. Now he was unraveling.

"She cares about you, Glenn. She stayed here two years for you. She'll come back. She probably just needs some time. It wears us out."

"Where would she go to rest? Can you take me there at least? So I can wait for her?"

"I can try to guess. Really, Glenn, it would be best if you just wait here. I'm sure she'll be back."

"But you said she'd be weak. What if she's hurt, or in trouble? What if . . ."

I finished the thought in my mind. *What if they don't let her come back.* Changelings, those that lived in the Wild all year round, were often kept as servants. I had managed to avoid it, I assumed, by not remaining in the forest. Ura was pretty, and sweet, and sylphs are fast messengers. She might have been noticed by something strong, something that would have the energy after the craziness of Midsummer to compel her to stay. I couldn't tell Glenn that. I didn't want to give him more to worry about. Sylphs were also quite difficult to catch. If she had even the slightest chance to get away, I was sure she would.

"If she goes anywhere to rest, it will probably be the cove she was born in." He had stopped pacing, so I moved closer and set my hand on his shoulder. "I really think you should stay here and wait. It won't be safe for you there." Glenn and I shared a human father. But his mother was an elf, and he could no more walk safely into the Wild than a nymph could walk out. Changelings could come and go, according to the treaty, for all the good it did us. We were little more than servants in either place.

"Then it won't be safe for her either. Come with me, help me find her." His gray eyes pleaded with me, his usually trumpeting voice weak and shaky.

"I can't Glenn, please." I wrapped my arms around myself and backed away from him. "I can't go back there right now."

"What am I supposed to do? Just sit around here and hope that she'll remember me?" He threw his hands up. "You never came back. Would you have come back this time if they hadn't come to get you?"

"I've gone back to Cyfar for years now. What difference does it make to you anyway? So what if I had come back to you. You'd just keep me locked up within those walls, just like you did to her." I stopped myself there, kept from yelling that I was glad she had gotten out and away from that life.

"Glade." Josie's voice was not loud, but we had trained under the same bard, and she could speak magic when she chose. That one word felt like a slap. Glenn and I turned to look at her. "Glade, I think you should go rest for now. Glenn, come sit down." Glenn tried to resist, but between the magic in her voice and the sternness of her eyes, he gave in and took a seat in the chair she offered. She came beside me and took my arm.

"I'm sorry," she said.

"It's fine. I'll make sure he eats something and gets some rest, too. But you need to get some more sleep and get back to yourself." She tugged at my blond hair.

I nodded and slipped away. She headed to the kitchen and Otsoa sat down at the table with Glenn. I didn't hear what they said, but it sounded like he was agreeing with me that going out after Ura was a bad idea. Glenn was not a Warden, and I could just imagine him getting lost out there looking for something impossible. I spent a few minutes trying to think of some way to help him before sleep came for me.

\#

I let myself rest completely in the room Josie gave me. My blond hair and freckled face melted away and I slept heavy and dreamless. When I woke, I took my time crafting my usual disguise, the one everyone in Cyfar thought was my real face, the one they thought of as Glade Balladeer. As I worked the magic, my face became a dark brown, my hair black and straight, the features on my face and the points of my ears softer. I changed back into my familiar, comfortable tunic and slacks. It was like sinking back into an old favorite chair; it just felt right.

When I came downstairs the dining room was quiet, dotted with a few people who were staying at the inn getting their breakfast. I didn't see Otsoa or Glenn, but I waved to Jose who was just coming out of the kitchen and found an empty linen-covered table away from the other diners. A small vase filled with silk flowers sat in the middle of the table, framed by two honey-colored candles. The only sounds were the whispers of conversation and occasional clinking of silverware or glasses. Taking a deep breath, I smelled warm bread and sharp herbs.

After making a sweep of the room Josie headed for my table. She was short, closer to dwarf height than halfling, and her features were rounder than most dwarves. She had told me when we met that there were halflings on her mother's side. We had been roommates in the home of our bard-mistress Delvine. A few glasses of her family's famous Vaster wine later and it felt like we had known each other for ages. So when she took a seat across from me and folded her hands neatly in front of her, I knew I was in trouble.

"Why aren't you helping your brother?" she asked.

I sighed. "It wouldn't do any good," I said. "We'd hunt up and down the coast for her, probably disturbing all kinds of Winter Wild which will start stirring now that Midsummer's passed, and not find a trace of her. She's part sylph; it's not like they leave tracks."

She didn't answer. Instead, she tilted her head and stared at me, the way she used to when I tried a new song out in front of her and she knew I hadn't practiced enough.

"They don't," I said. My voice grew higher as I tried to defend my claim. "You can't track them. Even if we could guess where she would be. I wake up in the most random places afterward."

Still Josie said nothing.

Finally, I looked down and started fiddling with the silverware. "I can't go back right now, Josie. I try to stay as far away as I can during this time."

Josie reached out her hand and set it on mine and squeezed it tight. "You're afraid you'll want to stay."

I nodded. "Yes. Glenn has helped me so much and I want to help him in return, I swear I do. But I can't risk that, not even for him. Not even for Ura."

"Do you really think she'll come back?"

"I don't know." I pulled my hand away. "I've never stayed, but I have a system. I don't know if Ura was even expecting to go this year. He managed to protect her for so long."

"Did he ever try to do that for you?"

My face twisted and I got a sour taste in my mouth. "Yes." It came out much more bitter than I had wanted. He had been trying to help in his own limited way. He knew I hated being called out there. "It didn't go well."

"Is that why you don't talk to him much?"

"That's hardly fair. He has his life, I have mine. We get together now and then—"

"When you need help," she interrupted.

"Look, he's a priest of Ventor, all right? They were designed to destroy the Wild. It's painful to visit him. I can only stand it for a few days at a time. And the one time he did try to keep me through Midsummer, he had to chain me in the cellar. I still managed to make the roots of some tree nearby break through the walls and freed myself. Nearly got him thrown out of the order."

Josie sat back as though I had slapped her. Her mouth gaped open and her eyes went wide. "Oh, Glade, I'm so sorry."

"Don't be. It's not your fault. It's not his fault. This is what I am. And it's best for everyone if I keep to myself as much as possible."

"You don't have a choice about it now," she said. She closed her mouth and set her jaw. "You are connected to Otsoa whether you like it or not. So you can't just keep to yourself anymore."

"Right." I picked at the tablecloth. I owed to her, and I owed it to the Lady to be more careful with this responsibility. The shame of not being there for them landed like a cold stone in my stomach. "Where is he, anyway?"

"He went with Glenn to see if there was anyone who would help them look for Ura."

"Oh, sure, a Warden would love to get sent on a hunt for a sylph Changeling."

"He thought maybe Roya would know someone. They went to message him."

That was a good move. If anyone would know who to hire for this sort of thing, it would be Roya. He had figured out that I was hiding my Wild nature and had hired Otsoa and me for the sort of jobs no other Warden would touch.

"Thanks for letting me stay here last night," I said after a long pause. "You didn't have to do that. I can pay for the room."

"Shut up," Josie said. "You never have to pay to stay here, or eat here, or any of that. Just do me a favor and figure out this thing with Otsoa, all right? Or we're going to have to build a pen for him out back."

"Well, at least then you could sell tickets. I doubt many in Casavera have seen a jaguar before."

"Sure, and we can end each show with you dropping your illusion and whipping the crowd into a frenzied dance. We'd sell out every night." It was good to see her smile, even if it was a tired one.

"How's your mom?"

"Doing well. They decided to go ahead and retire by the sea there. That's how I got the additional inn."

"Oh right. What's it called? Where is it?"

"It's up in Cyfar. The Branch and Vine. They do a lot of wine tastings and such. Still trying to get the hang of that." She lit up when she talked about it. I had worried when she left her bardic studies that she'd feel trapped working like this, but she seemed to be finding things to stay interested in.

"I'm sure it's going to be a huge success, just like this place."

Otsoa arrived then, without my brother, and joined us at the table. He tapped his fingers a few times, and I could see him calculating something behind his eyes. I'd known a lot of wizards, most of them cautious bookish sorts who did their tours at the towers out of duty and headed home as soon as possible. Otsoa was careful, most of the time. Now and then though, he would get this look in his dark eyes like he was searching through every possibility for the best one. Or the most exciting one.

"We got a message through to Roya. He seemed pleased that we got in touch with him," Otsoa said.

"Pleased? I should think he wouldn't want to be bothered. Unless he has a job for us." I groaned.

"Precisely. In exchange for finding someone to look for Ura, he asked that we take care of something for him. He wants us to meet with him tomorrow."

"Well, that's convenient. Just in time for me to check in to the Branch and Vine. We have some big tasting this weekend." Josie smiled at us. "Guess we are heading up to Cyfar."

Chapter Three

I wasn't sad to leave Casavera. It was quaint, but also snobby, assumed to be better than most other towns east of the Lumina River, even though it was where dishonored elven families came to live. Instead, I looked forward to being back in the bustling, modern, wide streets of Cyfar. The ride north in Josie's coach was smooth and pleasant, even if I did have to suffer through Josie and Otsoa's flirting.

Cyfar appeared on the horizon, tall and gleaming white, tiered marble steps draped with silk banners and hanging plants. At each corner a tower of darker stone marked the water screws that kept the canals flowing through the city. There was already a crowd gathering at the city gate, so our coach pulled into line to take our turn passing under the massive marble arches in the wall. Everything moved quickly and efficiently, and in less than thirty minutes we were rolling through the dark underside of Cyfar.

Everything smelly or dirty, involving sweat and hard work, was housed on the bottom level, including the stables. We parked the coach and headed to the closest canal. It would be pricier than the stairs, but it would be faster and easier to get to the upper levels.

"The Branch and Vine is on the fifth level," Josie said.

"I should probably check in at the Den," I said. "I know it's not as posh as your new place, but it's where I hang my guitar."

"Are you planning to stay there for the night then? Or should I find you a room?"

"Depends if Jinelle needs me to play tonight. I've been away for a bit, she may expect it." I wasn't looking forward to playing a long night at the Wyvern's Den, but it was how I paid for room and board.

"Oh let me come hear you play," Josie begged. "And I'd love to see the Den. You talk about it so much."

"You'll be disappointed, I'm sure." I looked at Otsoa. "Let her know you'd rather stay in comfort then hunker down with a bunch of retired Wardens."

"I don't know. I haven't slummed it in a while. And we have to be so proper and polite at Josie's places." He adopted a formal elvish accent. "Pass the salt, and dab the mouth and all that." He mimicked picking up a cup and sipping with his pinky up. Josie smacked his hand down.

"It'll be fun," Josie said. "We might even stay the night."

"I wouldn't subject you to that torture," I said, rolling my eyes. We loaded into a gondola and headed down the canal. It flowed into a large scoop attached to the water screw at the corner of the city. With a jolt we were swept up to the third level and dumped into another canal that we floated along until we pulled up beside the Wyvern's Den. The face of the building was made of unshaped dark stones. An old wooden sign swung over the door bearing a weathered red wyvern. The words 'historic charm in a modern district' were painted below it.

It was a bustling afternoon in the Den. Jinelle had redecorated again. This time the walls were lined with weapons, potion bottles, backpacks, anything typically carried by a Warden on their tours. The tables were still bare wood planks set on barrels, and it smelled of ale and sweaty leather.

"Glade, you're back!" Jinelle waved to me from behind the bar. "How was your tour?"

"Oh, the usual." I nodded to a few of the regulars seated at the bar, and Otsoa found a free table and pulled a chair out for Josie before settling down.

"Good to hear, good to hear. You're paid ahead through the end of the week, but if you have a night to spare to play, I won't complain."

I tried to calculate how much I had paid before I left. There were always stretches when I couldn't perform, and I tried to keep enough of what I made as a Warden to make up for it. I rarely had enough to cover it all, and I didn't remember having that much this time. But I wasn't going to argue.

"Would tomorrow night be all right? We just got back."

"Of course. You and your friends want dinner?"

"Yes, please." Everything felt so natural, as though I'd never left. I sighed and turned to join my friends. A woman was hovering around the table, standing a little too close to Otsoa. Josie was glaring up at her, but the woman had her back to me, so I couldn't tell if she noticed, or was just clueless.

"Are you sure, Master Ocelote, you look so very familiar. I'm sure I've met you back in Rheste. Hard to miss such a famed wizard," I heard the woman say as I inched up behind her. She was doing pretty well or would have been if Otsoa had been a typical human. The beads he wore on the two small braids in his hair bore the marks of the Ocelote family, and it was clear he was a wizard from the wands and pouches he wore at his belt. But he never used his family name, as it had been stripped from him the day he was thrown out of Rheste for using forbidden magic.

"It's no good, sweetie, you don't know this wizard," I said tapping her on the shoulder. "And I suggest you empty out your pockets." I wasn't certain she had been picking his pocket, but something in the way she moved and the ease with which she lied gave me a strong suspicion. She turned around to face me very slowly, and I readied to grab her or run after her if she decided to bolt.

"Glade?" she said. The moment I met her hazel eyes, I froze.

"Drinn?" I backed away from her a step. "What are you doing here?"

The expression on her face twisted from shock to disgust and she backed away as well. "I would ask you the same thing, if I cared enough to know the answer." She flicked a lock of glossy black hair over her shoulder and turned to leave.

"Not so fast." It took a lot of energy for me to cast a spell without music. I had to grasp the back of Otsoa's chair as I did it, but I forced Drinn to slow. She tried to keep walking, but it looked like she was pushing through deep mud. "Give it back."

"Glade," Otsoa said, starting to get up. "My gold is still—"

"Your gold is sure. But your spell powders aren't," I said. Otsoa's hand went to his belt and his face darkened. "Give them back," I repeated.

Drinn turned around, her muscles straining, still swamped by my spell. "Fine," she said through clenched teeth. "Here." She pulled a small pouch from her sleeve and dropped it on to the table, taking what felt like a full minute to complete the movement.

I didn't release her until Ostoa had taken up the pouch again. I expected her to run as soon as she was free, but she stayed there, staring at me as though I had a tree growing from the top of my head.

"So this is you now? Defending Wardens?" She said the word like it was the filthiest curse she knew. We didn't wear the badge when not on duty, but most people could tell a Warden when they saw one. I'd heard people say that spending that much time near the Wild made Wardens a little Wild themselves, when they thought there weren't any Wardens around to hear.

"Worse," I answered. "I am one."

"Hate to break up the reunion," Josie said and a cold chill spread over my skin. She had always been better at casting spells with her voice than I was. A

17

few ice crystals appeared in Drinn's hair. "But if you don't leave soon the Watch will have something to say about it."

Drinn laughed, waved her hand, and canceled Josie's spell. My surprise stopped me again. Drinn had been good at a lot of things when I'd known her, but magic was not one of them. "I'm not worried about the Watch. But you keep an eye on this one." Drinn pointed at me. "She's not great at hanging on to friends."

I don't think anyone had called for the Watch, but almost everyone in the Den was a Warden, or had been one, and they were starting to rise from their chairs and reach for their weapons. Drinn noticed, took one glance around the room, and shot me her old familiar smug grin. Then she vanished.

Two of the Wardens at the bar made random grabs at the space where she had been or would be if she had turned invisible and tried to escape the room, but they grabbed nothing but air. I sank into a chair at Otsoa's table, never taking my eyes from the spot she had vanished from.

"How did she do that?" I asked him. Invisibility was a tricky spell, and she would have still been stuck in the room with Wardens blocking the doors. Drinn hadn't just turned invisible, she had vanished.

"I have no idea," he answered. He sounded as shocked as I was. "But if she appears again anywhere in the city, the Watch will find her. I keep my bags coated with a special seeking powder. Her hand and her sleeve will be covered with it." He nodded to the Wardens who had tried to help and moved to the bar to buy them drinks.

"You all right?" Josie asked me.

"I think so." I kept my hands clenched together under the table. "Thanks for that."

"Anytime." She scratched at the table's rough surface. "I'm going to find the Watch, see if they can get on her trail." She was up and away from the table before she finished her sentence.

I got Jinelle's attention and asked for a mead, then changed my mind and ordered a bottle, hoping my hands would stop shaking before it arrived. Seeing Drinn again after all this time was bad enough, but finding that she was up to her old tricks with the addition of some new, unexplained magic made me queasy.

#

We didn't stay at the Den much longer. Once we had described Drinn to the Cyfar Watch, and Otsoa had given them some of his seeking powder to use in tracking her, we headed out, hoping to get away from the tension that was gripping us.

Another short boat ride up a few levels brought us to Josie's new inn, the Branch and Vine. The sun was getting low, filling the covered walks in darker shadows. The temperature fell too, and cool breezes floated in. The Branch and Vine was situated on a segment of the fifth level that had a large cutout, allowing people to get a glimpse of the garden on the level below. It made the whole area feel more open and peaceful, interrupting the typical traffic of the walks. The area of the railing in front of the inn was covered in grapevines.

"Josie," I said, turning a circle to take it all in. "This is breathtaking." They had several tables set out in front of the inn, and a large board showcasing their current wine offerings. "Really, you don't have to find a place for me here. I can go back to my room at the Den."

"Not with that sneak thief creeping around," Josie muttered as we went inside. She had met Drinn when I had, not long before she left her studies. She'd hated her instantly.

"You don't have to worry about her." I said with more conviction than I felt. There were a few people at the shiny dark wood bar sipping from tall glasses and nibbling on cheeses, but it didn't look like dinner service had started yet.

"You've said that before," Josie stopped in the center of the room and turned to face me. She had set her jaw again and looked up at me with narrowed eyes.

"Is she going to be a problem?" Otsoa asked. "I can be more aggressive about pressing charges when they find her."

"No need for all that. She'll skip town soon anyway, now that so many Wardens know she's here." I glanced up at the ceiling painted with scenes from old stories, knights in armor parading on horseback and carrying long banners.

"Does she know?" Josie whispered.

"No." I snapped my head to her look at her. "No, I never told her." I didn't need to clarify what. I would never have told Drinn what I was. I would never have told anyone if I hadn't needed to. "But she does know a lot of other things."

19

"I bet she does." Josie led us to a back room, something meant for private dinners, and waved for us to sit down. "You used to get up to all sorts of trouble in those days."

"Right, not as though anyone else here is hiding something illegal," I said, staring pointedly at Otsoa. He shook his head and took a seat. Between my heritage and his shape-shifting, we would have worse consequences than a simple street thief.

"There's illegal, and then there's wrong," Josie said.

"Well, most of the world doesn't see a difference." I sighed and sagged into a chair. "Just let her be. She'll fleece a few foolish people into giving up their wealth and then be on her way."

"Glade, what is going on with you?" Josie leaned on the table to look down at me. "You wouldn't have said that before—"

I shot her a glare and knew from the shock in her eyes that it was too strong. But it was unfair of her to throw that in my face. Maybe Midsummer did do things to me, but it's not as though I had a choice. After two weeks of that music flowing through my mind, I was fortunate I wasn't still dancing around trying to seduce people with my flute. She brushed past me and walked out the door, mumbling something about checking the dinner reservations and slammed the door behind her.

"I haven't known you nearly as long as she has," Otsoa said, his voice soft. "But she's right. You wouldn't have said something like that three weeks ago. Being around good friends was good for you."

I rolled my eyes. "Let's not get into that right now."

He pressed his lips together but changed the subject. "The way she vanished like that," Otsoa mused, tapping his fingers on the table. "She didn't just turn invisible. There were too many people for her to slip past that way. Does she use portals, like you do?"

"The Ways? I doubt it. She didn't have to sing or speak to get them to open. And those are only at fixed locations, not the middle of random taverns. Whatever it is, it's new. She couldn't do that when I knew her. It's probably some kind of illusion, combined with speed?" I shrugged.

"It happened too fast for me to see what she did. Probably had a strong charm on her of some kind." He thought over it a little longer and then shook his head. "Anyway, while we have a minute, we should talk." He pointed again to his pendant.

I sighed. "So I can tell when you want to change," I said. "Makes me queasy. And I can keep you from changing. And get you to come back to being human."

"Though I haven't fought you on it, so we don't know how well. And I can feel when you go Wild," he said with a quick smile. I didn't return it. "And I may be able to help restrain you too, if I was prepared for it." His smile faded.

"But it doesn't make you sick? That doesn't seem fair."

"I get nauseous when I change. It wasn't pleasant when you first went out. I mean, it felt like something was dragging me outside of myself."

"It's not like we can experiment with this. I take no pleasure in 'going Wild' as you put it. I mean, it's pleasurable, but also disturbing. There's no control at all."

"I know what you mean. When I'm a beast there's none of my reason to govern my choices, nothing stopping me from doing whatever I feel like doing. And though I know I would never hurt Josie willingly, I was becoming afraid that something might happen."

My jaw tightened and I pushed down a chill of fear. If any harm came to Josie from his actions or mine, I would never forgive myself. I knew he wouldn't either. The pendant had been a gift from the Lady, something I thought would keep him in human form, and I had wanted that for Josie and for him. I hadn't known it would tie us together so strongly.

"So we just have to do what we can to keep each other under control," I said, forcing my hands open. I had clenched them tight enough to leave dimples in my palm.

"Right, I agree." He looked away. "I have been much better, since you did that for me. I guess I don't have to explain to you how terrifying it is to feel your own mind slipping away."

"Yes, I know." I held out my hand to him. "Here's to keeping each other in our right minds."

He took my hand and shook it. "And in our right shapes," he added.

Chapter Four

Our appointment with Roya wasn't until mid-morning, allowing me to sleep in, then enjoy a mug of coffee in my room. The room Josie let me use—she still refused to let me pay—was small and cozy and smelled like roses. I splayed myself out on the creamy sheets and then changed my mind, worried I would spill coffee all over them. Instead, I sat at the small desk beside the bed and rubbed my feet into the thick carpet. Though I had been hired for a few jobs in the upper levels of Cyfar, I had never stayed there overnight. I was going to miss this.

I wandered downstairs and found Otsoa sitting at the bar. Glenn was sitting beside him. I hesitated in the archway that divided the tasting area from the dining room and tried to catch Otsoa's attention. He was turned away from me. His long black hair obscured most of his face and his hands were tracing shapes on the bar. Glenn followed the motions with his eyes.

"Well that seems needlessly complicated," Glenn said, waving his hands over Otsoa's as though to brush away whatever he was trying to demonstrate.

"And that was only level one," Otsoa said, laughing. "The patterns they showed us in our fourth year wouldn't fit in this room."

"And they expect you to keep all of that in your head? No wonder spellcasting takes so long." Glenn shook his head and caught sight of me, his face falling from amusement to a false calm. I preferred it much more when he was openly angry. This attempt to keep emotion from his face made him look like he was wearing a mask.

"Good morning," I said softly.

Otsoa turned and waved me over. "Good morning," he said. "You look better this morning."

"I just needed to get some more sleep." I cast a cautious glance at Glenn. "Sorry about yesterday."

"So am I." He slipped off the stool and pulled me into a hug. "I'm glad you came back safe." He pulled back, his hands on my shoulders, and looked into my eyes.

I had to look away. "I'm sorry about Ura. If anyone can help you find her it will be Roya. He's got connections everywhere. I just, I just can't—"

"I know, and I shouldn't have expected you to want to go back. I have no idea what kind of strength it takes for you to escape." He squeezed my arm and moved aside so I could join them at the bar. "Ventor knows I could never keep you from it."

"I don't think Ventor planned for people like me to exist." I slumped on to the stool. Glenn frowned at me, and I hoped he took my statement as an expression of my current mood and not a start to a debate. We'd argued about it before, and he always insisted the god he followed had a plan for helping Changelings as well. He speculated the knowledge had been lost during the Fairy Wars. I assumed there were those Ventor had broken free hundreds of years ago, and those he had left Wild, and that was that. Those of us who came after were left to fend for ourselves.

Glenn started to say something, stopped himself, and sighed. "Thank you both for taking a job from Roya in exchange for his help for me. I hope you don't get tasked with anything too dangerous."

"Last time he just sent us to a garden party," Otsoa quipped. That was a gross understatement of our first mission together. "Can't get much worse than that."

"Your ride's here," Josie said, swinging the front door open. Three men carrying large casks trooped in before a shorter man in a red tunic entered. Josie stopped at the bar and hugged Otsoa. "Will you be back before you leave? Or should I wish you good luck now?"

"They usually give us some time to get ready," Otsoa answered, kissing the top of her head. "We'll be back."

Josie turned to me. "You take care of him, all right?"

"Of course." That was all the time she had for me. She hurried off to fuss at the cask carriers and direct them where to set her wares.

The gentleman in the red tunic cleared his throat. "I have a boat outside for you," he said with a wave at the door. "Roya expects you to arrive on time."

Glenn, Otsoa and I followed him out and piled into a sleek gondola. I had expected it to be red as well, as Roya had a flair for showing off just how much he could afford with such an elite color. The slender boat was tastefully painted a rich brown gold with flowers carved along the edges. It carried us up to the top level of the city.

Everything on the top level was pristine. The sidewalks were spotless white, the buildings shining, so much that the lawn and manicured bushes looked like dark smudges in comparison. The last time we had visited, the cool breezes here had been a relief, but at the height of summer, it was blazing hot. Long awnings had been unfurled over the sidewalks, and massive tents were set up on most of the lawns. A few of those lucky enough to live up here were lounging in the shade they provided.

Roya's palazzo stood near the center of the level, surrounded by a low wall covered in parts with thick vines. We were led through a citrus orchard, shaded by branches heavy with oranges and lemons. Our guide stopped and looked around as though he had expected someone else to be there, then sighed.

"My master requires all visitors to be visible before they are allowed to enter." His voice was weary as though he had made the same announcement many times before.

"What happens once we enter?" Drinn asked, appearing from the shadows beside a tree. I sputtered, wanting to say several nasty comments but they all crowded my mouth at once. Glenn started, and Otsoa rolled his eyes.

"What are you doing here?" I finally managed to spit out.

Drinn wrinkled her face in our direction. "Working, same as you."

"If you enter while invisible" —our guide droned on—"things will become very unpleasant for you very quickly. The master has a strong protection spell over the whole house. I would rather not have to clean up such a mess today, if it's all the same to you."

Drinn narrowed her eyes at him. "Very well. I promise to stay visible."

"Then follow me please."

My stomach dropped. Whatever she was doing now, it was clear she was no Warden, and was not licensed to get hired by a legitimate questfinder like Roya. I had not known Roya long, but the jobs he was known for were beyond reproach. It was part of why his name had gotten us so far on all our jobs for him. Working for Roya usually meant going after the most frightening of Wild creatures, and he only chose the best to work for him. Though they may not all survive, they would ensure the job was done before they died.

When I had initially been approached by him, I'd thought it was a joke, there was nothing I could be useful for on a job like that. For Otsoa and I, he'd had something different in mind, something most Wardens would not have agreed to. But since he knew our secrets, we hadn't had much choice. It turned out I was glad to have been on that job, glad to have been able to help save other Changelings from a different kind of monster. But no matter how rough the job, I couldn't believe Roya would turn to the likes of Drinn.

#

He led us to the side entrance, the same way I had visited before. I wondered if anyone ever used the massive front doors at the top of the wide marble stairs that faced the street. We passed through dim hallways lined with paintings and ended up in the office where I had first met Roya. The room was darker than I remembered. There were no windows, only three globes lit by magic, floating by the ceiling. Rather than bright yellow, they glowed a muddy orange, casting a warm light over the bookshelves and the massive desk that dominated the far side of the room.

Roya stood to one side of the desk, and another man stood on the other. Roya, a stout older elf clearly used to the finest things in life, was draped in his usual dyed red robes, not the cheap cloth under an illusion color spell. The other man looked meager in comparison, a tall slender human wearing tight black pants and a black flowing shirt. He even had a black feather in his hat. Black was the only dye that rivaled red for expense, and I wondered if the man wore it on purpose to show off for Roya.

"Ah, here they are," Roya said as we entered. "Meet Glade Balladeer, and Otsoa Stranero. I see your own applicant has arrived as well." He directed this last at Drinn. She was looking over the shelves with a scrutiny that mirrored an appraiser checking over jewelry.

The man in black nodded at Drinn, and she returned the gesture.

Glenn stepped forward and bowed to Roya. "Thank you again, sir, for offering your help. I didn't know what I was going to do."

"It is a small price to pay for the service of these two Wardens." Roya nodded at Otsoa and I. I was flattered.

"You mean you aren't getting paid for this?" Drinn muttered to me. She was standing a little too close to my left. I ignored her. The man in black chuckled.

I looked over the man in black again. Roya had a reputation for the best and most successful jobs, but also for the utmost discretion. All of the jobs I had been hired for included secrecy clauses, not the kind of thing I expected he would want a guest overhearing.

"Who are you?" I asked him.

"I'm Negri," he answered and made a fancy flourishing bow, sweeping his hat off his head so that the feather brushed the floor. He popped the hat back on at a jaunty angle. "I'm your new boss." His voice was low and gravelly, like someone scraping metal over stone.

"That was not the agreement." I was about to step forward and make my opinion clearer to this black-clad stranger, but Otsoa caught my arm and kept me in place.

"True, you agreed to do a job for me in exchange for helping Glenn. But I owe Negri a favor. And he was looking for someone with your expertise." Roya's voice was like a bell ringing over the sea, clear and steady. But I wasn't reassured. I glanced sharply at Roya, wondering if he had revealed my secret to Negri as well. Roya had originally gotten me to work for him because he had found out that I was a Changeling. Was that why Negri wanted to hire me?

Roya shook his head in response to my glance, a very small gesture. I felt a little relieved, but only a little. I didn't know this Negri, and I didn't trust him.

"He's not the worst boss I've ever worked for," Drinn commented.

"If you're the sort of person he usually hires, I don't think we'll be a very good fit for the job," Otsoa said. He was also casting a wary glance at Negri. Glenn was turning red, and his lips were pressed tightly together.

"Why don't you and I carry on our conversation in another room," Roya said, coming to stand beside Glenn and setting a hand on his arm. "We have a lot to discuss, and the technicalities involved in setting up these jobs can be so tedious."

Glenn hesitated. "Glade . . ."

"It's fine, Glenn. We'll meet up after." I tried to sound confident, but it came out more urgent. I didn't want my brother anywhere near this man or his probably illegal business offer. Glenn left with Roya.

"Roya tells me you have more knowledge about the Wild than most," Negri said once they were gone. "And this one," he nodded to Drinn, "says you have some sort of connection. That you know when they are nearby?"

I nodded but didn't speak. I wasn't giving him anything if I didn't have to.

"Good. And you," Negri turned to Otsoa. "I hear you have learned ways to cast spells more quickly, to take more creative routes to the same results?"

"I've improvised here and there." Otsoa shrugged. "Don't know how noteworthy it is."

"Humble lot." He sat on Roya's desk.

"And what is she here for?" Otsoa pointed at Drinn. She blew a kiss back at him. "She's wanted by the Watch for theft."

"You will need an expert thief. And I have made arrangements with the Watch," Negri answered. I was about to ask him for more details on his arrangement, but he continued. "Tell me, oh great Wild loremaster, what do you know about goblins?"

"Oh no, you have to be joking." I threw my hands up and paced over to a bookshelf. "Let's skip the amusements at our expense and talk about the real job."

"No joke," Negri said. "Goblins. What do you know?"

I peered at him, trying to guess if he was serious, and how much he might already know. The Wardens and people like Roya knew some things about the Wild, but it was in bits and pieces, just what they ran into while working their jobs. Clerics could know more if they bothered reading anything in their libraries, but much of that knowledge had been taken away and hidden during the Fairy Wars, so it was also incomplete. But the goblins were another story entirely, something that was mere rumor, even among clerics and their librarians.

"I thought there weren't any goblins anymore," Otsoa said. "They disappeared before the Wars."

"Not exactly," I answered. "They went into hiding during the Wars. Not that they were very out in the open before that. Goblins were Wild, and then were exiled. They lived in a city as far from the forests as they could go, somewhere underground, and would come out now and then to get food or steal children."

"Stealing children is nothing new for the Wild. Exiled for what?" Otsoa still sounded puzzled.

"No one knows. But the Wild loves keeping its hold on everything it can. If it purposely exiled a whole city of people, they must have done something pretty bad." I ran my fingers along the spines of Roya's books. "Not that it matters. No one knows where the Goblin City is."

"No one *knew*," Negri corrected. He slid off the desk and hurried around it to pull a roll of paper from a drawer. He unfurled it across the desk with a snap. "Until now."

The map was crude, hand drawn with a thick, soft charcoal, and was smudged badly across the right side. The top left was marked with a drawing that could have been a grid of buildings or a poorly drawn maze and was marked as the Goblin City. Nearby, separated from the city by a thick swath of forest, was a clear depiction of a Warden tower, labeled simply 'North Tower.'

"This just keeps getting better," I mumbled.

"That's not a short journey, or an easy one," Otsoa said, examining the map. "There's a lot of rough country between here and what's left of the North Tower."

"That's why Roya suggested I hire the two of you," Negri said. He leaned back on the desk again and smiled at us. "I have heard such great things."

"You would have done better to hold out for a fighter or two, and at least another wizard." I turned away from the map and from all of them. I didn't want them to see my hands were starting to shake.

"Fighters are so clunky and noisy, and are terrible at sneaking," Negri said. He rolled up the map and handed it to Drinn. "And wizards, though generally useful in border skirmishes, don't tend to travel well. All those dusty books and bottles of powders. No, once I heard about the two of you, I knew I had finally found the perfect adventurers for this job."

Sure, the perfect adventurers. A wizard who shouldn't have a license and a Changeling that shouldn't be working anywhere better than the bottom level of the city. Roya may not have told Negri our secrets, but he may have told Negri that he had something on us, something that would keep us from refusing.

"What are we stealing?" I asked. I tried to keep my voice steady.

"Drinn knows the details. What you recounted to us about the goblins was accurate, but not complete. It was the fault of the goblins that the North Tower fell. They clearly have a very powerful weapon, and the Wardens can never reclaim that tower until we take it from them. Or, at least, disable it." Negri exchanged a long glance with Drinn when he finished. I wasn't buying it. This is the kind of job Roya would have sent us on. There was no reason for this underground skullduggery. But at this point, I didn't want to know, and Otsoa seemed convinced. If we were just escorting a thief to this mythical city and back, it was more than a fair exchange for Roya helping my brother find his lost love.

\#

We went through the usual paperwork, though we weren't bound to secrecy about this job, as I was used to when working for Roya. There was no point in forcing our silence, as no one would believe what we were up to.

Once they were gone, Negri gathered the papers and tucked them away in the desk, then opened another drawer and presented Otsoa with a large leather bag. Otsoa placed it on the table and began inspecting it. It had several flaps that overlapped, each lined with small pockets and bands stuffed with bottles and packets of all sorts of things, some of which I had never heard of. Whatever qualms Otsoa may have had about this job were buried under an eager grin as he rooted through the bag, taking out a tube or packet to examine the contents more closely.

"Is this what I think it is?" Otsoa held up small jar filled with a sparkling white powder.

"What do you think it is?" Negri asked, grinning.

"Unicorn horn?" Otsoa guessed. He sounded cautious, but hopeful.

I looked to Negri for the answer as well.

"It is," Negri said. He put on a solemn look, but his eyes still gleamed. "Not much of that left in Drakir. I do my best to keep a small supply."

"Do you have any idea what I can do with just a pinch of this?" Otsoa wiggled the bottle so the powder clouded up inside, then floated back down to the bottom. "Do you give this to everyone who works for you?"

"Only the special ones," Negri answered. He turned his attention to me. "Wizards are so easy to please. I take much more joy in outfitting bards. So many more options."

I didn't like his tone, but I couldn't pinpoint why. His smile was twisted and unwelcoming. "Funny. We don't really need much more than our voice."

"You say that," he replied. "But I know where to find all the good toys." He held out a rolled-up cloth, about as long and thick as his arm.

"What's this?"

"Finest constructed instruments, tuned by dwarves in the caves in Hakvar, tested by Nicolli himself."

I took the roll and gently unfurled it on the desk. It held a set of crystal flutes in different sizes, tucked into long narrow pockets in the roll. They glinted in the orange light. It was a rich gift, more than worth what Roya had paid for our last job.

"You do know how impractical these things are on the field, right?" I asked, as I ran my hands lightly over each one. They were perfectly smooth. "If they make it to the Goblin City without breaking, which I can't guarantee, I'd have to have my hands free to use them and have enough time to think about which is the best to use in the moment. I'd rather just use my voice."

He frowned, just a quick downturn of his lips before his oily smile returned. "Well, if you would rather not have those." He shrugged and leaned past me to roll the cloth back up again.

"I'd rather not take anything out that I can't be sure I'll bring back in one piece. It's why I don't usually take my guitar into rough country either."

"Hm. Well, perhaps you would prefer something more rugged then."

He put the roll back into the closet at the back of Roya's study. It felt strange watching him root through someone else's things, or perhaps Roya had allowed him space there to store supplies. I didn't like the thought that they worked together that often. He came back to the desk and set down a long thin box of rough wood and flipped the lid open to reveal a small silver flute. It had a few dings on the surface but had been polished to a shine.

"May I?" I asked, picking it up.

"Just no drowsiness spells, if you don't mind. They give me a headache," Negri said, raising a thin hand to his temple.

I nodded and lifted the flute to my lips. The holes were well spaced and easy to cover, and it was very light so probably not solid silver, only plated. Even better. I played a long low note and then tripped lightly up a scale to see how high it would go before sounding shrill. The notes remained smooth and mellow even into the highest register. The ruffles on Negri's shirt rustled as I called up a quick breeze with the music.

"This is perfect. And I'm sure I can bring it back in once piece. Even if it gets damaged it can probably be repaired, more easily than those others."

"No need," Negri said, waving his hand over it like it smelled bad. "You can keep that."

I gripped the flute to my chest and grinned. "Thanks!"

"You are a very odd bard," he said.

"I know," I replied proudly.

He was frowning again. "I can see why Roya chose the two of you. So fastidious. Take the rest of the day to get packed. I will arrange transportation for you as far as Rhiodeja, but you will have to head north on your own after that. Tonight, enjoy dinner at your friend's inn. My treat."

I narrowed my eyes at him. "You don't think we're coming back from this, do you? Is that why you're being so generous?"

"I have full faith in your abilities to get into and out of the Goblin City in safety." He leaned forward and the gleam in his eyes brightened even more—perhaps just a trick of the strange lighting in the room. "If you bring back what I'm asking for, it will be worth every last magic item in Drakir."

Drinn had remained very quiet in the corner through all this. He didn't bring out anything for her, but it seemed they had been talking before this. Perhaps she had gotten her gift then. Was he the reason she was suddenly so magically talented?

Another servant escorted us out of Roya's palazzo and back to the garden.

"So what's the arrangement you have with Negri?" I asked Drinn.

"What's this arrangement you have with Roya?" she shot back.

I rolled my eyes. "There aren't any outstanding warrants for my arrest," I pointed out. "What's to stop us from calling the Watch for you now?"

"Negri has his fingers in just as many pies and has secrets about just as many important people in this town as Roya does. That's all you need to know." She bobbed a sarcastic curtsy and vanished again.

Chapter Five

Otsoa kept his new pack tucked tightly on his lap on the boat ride back to the Branch and Vine. He waited until we had dropped down and away from the top level, then looked me in the eyes.

"All right, how bad is this, really?" He patted the bag. "They don't give out supplies like this without a reason."

"True." I sighed. "I don't know much more about goblins than what I said in there. They were Wild, they were exiled, and they've been underground for ages."

"But I've heard stories of kids being taken by goblins in Rheste. If their city is up by the North Tower, how is that possible?"

"Probably just stories." I shrugged. At least, that's what I was hoping. If the goblins had a way of getting around all of Drakir without giving away where they were hiding, they may have discovered the Ways as well. "Maybe they just want us prepared for the rough traveling on the way there. No one's been up that way since the tower fell, so who knows what is living around it now."

"You don't think we should just take one of your portals up there from Rhiodeja? It would make the going easier."

"There would have to be a Way already in place. I can't make one myself if I haven't been to the destination. But I could find out if there is an existing one." It would mean pestering Glenn and maybe visiting his library again. He was the only one I knew who had ever found a book showing the network of invisible portals that stretched across Drakir, a leftover from the days when the clerics of Ventor needed to travel quickly to fight back the Wild.

"It's worth a try. The less time spent in rough country with a sneaky thief the better."

"Look, I get it, she's a thief, all right? It's not like she's going to stab us all in our sleep and run off with your unicorn powder."

"No, just knock us all out with some spell and vanish into the wilderness. Why do you defend her?" He reached over the side of the boat and splashed a handful of water at me.

"Hey!" I splashed back. "She got me through some tough times, all right?"

"Well we're not telling her about the unicorn powder, or any of the other goodies in the bag."

"We're not telling her about anything," I said, suddenly serious.

"She really doesn't know about what you are?"

"Not a thing. And I'd like it to stay that way." We pulled up in front of the Branch and Vine, but I waited, watching Otsoa for a response.

He blinked his dark eyes at me, his brows pressed together. "All right. No problem."

Josie came out to meet us at the boat. She had changed into a long gown, colored a deep pink, fit tight and high on her waist and flowing out around her legs. Her hair was up in a fancy array of braids and pinned with pearls.

"I don't know what you promised to do for Roya, but you could eat here free for a week and my uncle wouldn't bat an eye," she said.

Otsoa hopped out of the boat and pulled her into a hug. "Hello, beautiful." He kissed the top of her forehead. "Where is your uncle, anyway?"

"Why?" She peered up at him, and he waggled his eyebrows at her. "Oh really? Tonight? Can't we just have a peaceful dinner together?"

"Come on, it won't take that long, and it's been over a week since the last time. I don't want him to think my interest has waned." He tucked her arm under his and started pulling her toward the inn.

"What's going on?" I asked. I hopped out of the boat, had to hop back in to get the box with the flute inside, and hurried to catch up to them.

"You don't have to do this at all. It's so old fashioned," Josie whined. "Uncle Joff will be busy in the wine cellar now, and he'll get all grumpy."

"Nonsense. He loves it."

I followed them inside, where Joff was already at the wine counter, setting out various bottles. He was incredibly delicate with each bottle, though he was a bulky, muscular dwarf with arms like gnarled tree roots. Otsoa took a moment to straighten his tunic, adjust his belt, and flatten his hair before striding up to the counter. Joff glanced at him but went back to lining up the bottles.

"*Herre hovding*," Otsoa said, bowing deeply to Joff. "I would like to present another gift to prove to you my sincere love and devotion to your *larling* and niece Johanna von Fennelling, for whom my heart smolders like a phoenix."

Joff let out a heavy sigh and came around the counter, his eyes fixed on Otsoa who was still bent over in a bow. Otsoa's head was just level with Joff's now. Josie was standing nearby, her head slightly bent, but she was blushing all the way to her ears.

"All right, let's see it," Joff grunted.

Otsoa straightened and moved away from the counter to one of the high bistro tables. He cleared off the flower vase and glasses, pulled a wand from his belt, and began a complicated spell.

I loved watching spellcasters work. Artificers like myself could do magic, but only simple, short-lived spells. It was great if you needed something fast and direct. But a true wizard could do some amazing things, given enough time and the right materials. The end of Otsoa's wand was fitted with a convex lens, tinted light blue. The wand itself was a dark polished wood, though the polish was worn in parts.

Otsoa moved the wand into place and a thin ray of blue light shot out and hit the table. There was no effect, but it stayed in place even when Otsoa moved his wand to another angle. Soon he had five beams of light pointed at the table forming the corners of a pentagon. Once the lights were in place, he tucked the wand back into his belt and took out a small vial. He tipped five drops of the clear liquid on to the table. The incantation was a mixture of elvish and dwarvish words. As he chanted, the beams on the table twisted as though the top ends were attached to a wheel, and the bottom ends to the same point under the table. As the beams slid aside, a gold-rimmed plate appeared. Otsoa waved his hands and the beams disappeared. He lifted the plate so Josie could see it.

"It's beautiful," Josie said, clasping her hands. Joff examined the plate closely, running his fingers over the intricate painting on the front. I had seen plates like that before, only in Josie's parents' house. Vines twisted around the rim, and the center held a portrait of Josie surrounded by dainty flowers. The paint was glazed into the clay of the plate, bright blues and greens and glimmering golds.

"Impressive," Joff said. "Do you accept it?" He looked over at Josie.

She rolled her eyes and nodded. "You already know that, Uncle Joff."

"Your dwarvish pronunciation is improving," Joff said to Otsoa. "Very well, I am convinced you truly love her and are able to provide for her."

"Not like he'll need to," Josie mumbled.

34

"Now we have only to meet with your family." Joff turned back to Otsoa.

"Yes, sir. I have written to them." Otsoa held Joff's gaze, but he shifted his weight uneasily. "I have not heard back yet. But Rheste is a long way off."

Joff narrowed his eyes but nodded after a moment. "True enough. You let me know as soon as you hear."

"Of course, sir," Otsoa bowed again.

"We have a table set up for you in the back." Joff pointed toward the back room. "Full wine service to be included. Enjoy your dinner."

#

Otsoa and I had enjoyed dinner at Josie's first inn, the Fonte, several times when we had been working in Casavera. The Branch and Vine made that look like a fireside cookout. There were six courses, including a full pasta course which was a rare delight. The wine was delectable, and by the dessert course, we were all more than merry. Glenn arrived halfway through the first course but didn't stay through the whole night. In the break between the last course and dessert, I walked him to the door.

"You can stay the night, you know, and head back in the morning," I said while we waited for a canal boat to pick him up.

"I'm only going to Casavera. And you know how sleepy wine makes me." He finished his sentence with a yawn. The sunset tinted the canal water purple and spread deep shadows under the colonnades.

"I still don't like you traveling alone."

"I'm a cleric, Glade. If anything comes after me, I'll set it on fire." He wiggled his right hand at me, and I flinched away. I knew he wouldn't use a fire spell now, in front of me. Even the thought of Ventor's fire sent terror into the center of me, harsher than any arrow. He frowned. "Sorry."

"No, I, it's fine." I took a deep breath and calmed myself. This was my brother, I reminded myself. I'd known him for years, one of the few who had known what I was from the moment he met me. He had been there for me after I had lost control and gone Wild at the wrong times. But now and then it terrified me to know what he could do.

We stood silently, breathing in the damp air and listening to the soft hiss of the water in the canal. Things always ended up like this. We would fall silent, and eventually I would get on with my life and he would get on with his. Until I needed him to hide me again. At least now I knew a much faster way to travel to him. One of the Ways opened directly into the library of his church.

"By the way, could you look something up for me when you get home? Find out if there was a Way that went to the North Tower."

"The North Tower?" He scrunched his mouth back and forth in thought. He made the funniest faces when he was thinking. "I don't think there was. It may have fallen before they discovered that magic. But I'll take a look." He raised an eyebrow and glared at me. "How bad is it, really? What did that man hire you to do? I know you're doing this to help me out, but if it's the kind of thing they're willing to hire a criminal like Drinn for—"

"I'm not only doing this for you." I folded my arms and looked out over the canal. "Roya knows what I am. I pretty much have to take any job he offers."

"Glade, you don't have to." He set his hand on my shoulder. "We could find sanctuary for you somewhere."

"No, thank you." I leaned in and nudged him. "We know how well that goes."

Glenn pulled me into a hug and squeezed my shoulders. "I'm going to find a way to help you, if I have to read every last dusty book in Drakir."

My heart skipped and I jerked back enough to look up at him. "You have not been looking through all those old books to . . . You said you were trying to find a way to protect against the attacks that were happening."

"That was a nice side effect," he shrugged. "But I have to believe Ventor taught the old clerics something to help. Something better than keeping you locked away."

"Don't, Glenn. Please don't drive yourself crazy trying to save me from the Wild." I squeezed his arm and shook him a little. "That's a rabbit hole I don't want to lose you in. Things are fine. I'm fine."

"Fine isn't good enough." A boat arrived, bumping hollow against the side of the canal. He hopped on and settled into the cushioned seat at the back end. "We're going to make this better. Just wait."

I watched the boat glide away and disappear into the shadows. I hadn't asked him if he had gotten into trouble for giving me sanctuary any of the times that he had taken me in. I assumed that because he ran his own small church, perhaps they didn't watch him so closely, but I knew from experience not everyone in the Church of Ventor felt the same pity for Changelings as my brother did. Still, I would have said a prayer to Ventor for the safe return of Ura, if I thought that was the kind of thing Ventor would do.

"So you're going off on another job with Drinn?" Josie's voice echoed under the colonnade. I turned to find her peering around one of the columns, her pink dress a dusky purple in the darkness.

"Yes, I am. But not because I want to." I leaned against the cool marble column. The first stars were appearing in the blue-black sky. "Thanks for coming to get me, by the way. It was much nicer coming home with friends."

"Anytime."

"So, things got serious pretty quickly with you and Otsoa." I was tired of this job already, without having set foot on the trail yet. I thought we could both use something more cheerful to talk about.

"Nothing goes quickly when you're talking about dwarvish courtship." She started pulling the pearl hairpins from her braids, letting her hair fall around her shoulders. "This was only the beginning phase, doing enough to show my uncle he has a steady income and wasn't just a fly-by-night suitor."

"I hope he's convinced you of that, too."

She blushed and tucked the pearl pins into the bodice of her gown. I had always been jealous of how well she filled out the current fashions, her curves highlighted by the high waists and flowing skirts. And I had never been able to tuck anything away in my bodice, not without it slipping through and getting caught at my waistband.

"It didn't take much convincing," she admitted. "I still find it hard to believe, but I'm not going to argue if he wants to stick around. I just didn't expect he'd go all out and fulfill every custom my uncle asked of him. I mean, did you hear him speaking dwarvish?"

"He's pretty good. What's the next phase?"

"Meeting with his family." She tilted her head and looked up at me. "You haven't ever heard him mention them, have you?"

"No, sorry."

"I gathered they're not on speaking terms. Not since he started turning into a big cat."

"There's a chance they still want to connect with him, that he was taken from them. And now that things are more under control they might answer."

"I guess we'll find out." She buried her face in her hands and then looked up again, smiling. It was her 'I have a customer' smile. "I told him I don't care.

37

I don't care if Uncle Joff approves of him or his family or any of it. Well, I mean, I care if mother approves. But they won't come back to meet him until Uncle Joff signs off on things." She let out a long sigh and her smile melted away. "It's kind of a mess."

I looped my arm around her neck and leaned down to speak into her ear. "That's exactly how it should be. Only the light fragile nothings don't make a mess. The big heavy important things leave a mess behind."

She giggled. "Then me and you are what, a full-on fire-breathing dragon?"

"That we are."

#

We gathered outside the west gate of Cyfar, the sun up enough to paint the sky pink and gold, but the city walls were covered in shadow. I shivered as we waited in line. Negri had secured us seats on the railway between Cyfar and Rhiodeja. It was one of the few modern conveniences that made me truly uncomfortable. They had laid down the long stretch of wooden rails a few years ago and trained massive work horses to pull cars back and forth between the two cities. At first it was only for trade, sending grain and lumber over from the east, and bringing back coffee, wine, cloth and other finery from the west. They had only just started taking passengers.

Within the cities, the feeling of the Wild calling to me was quiet, barely a whisper. But it was still there. There were plants and animals and other natural things still around, even if they were tamed. The only two places where I felt completely disconnected from it was in a church of Ventor, and on a rail car. Something about being off the ground and shut off from everything living around us cut the Wild off from me. It was a comfort for a few hours, but the missing of it, the hole that it left in me, started to gape after that, until I felt like I would be swallowed up by it. It was why I couldn't stay with Glenn long, even though he offered to keep me safe. And why I was glad it was not a long trip to Rhiodeja by rail.

Drinn appeared as the conductor called the final boarding. One moment we were surrounded by porters loading luggage, the next she was standing beside me, staring up at the rail car.

"I've never been on one of these before," she said. "Are those two horses really going to pull all this?"

"They say the wheels run easier along rails than they would on a road," I answered. "I've seen them do it. Rode out to Rhiodeja once for my last Warden test. Besides, did you notice the driver?"

She leaned back so she could see the young man attending the horses, then clicked her tongue. "Huh. A Changeling?"

I shivered at the contempt in her voice. "Right. He can keep the horses refreshed, get them more energy as we travel." The young man had spiky dark hair and a long face. The conductor spoke sharply to him, and the young man shrank away. He would be watched closely and fired at the slightest infraction. I'd lived through one job under those conditions, then promised myself I would do anything I had to in order to get a real job.

"Well, let's enjoy the comfort while we have it. The road north won't be so nice." She ran her eyes along the car, then to the car behind. The second car was getting loaded with crates, chests, and carefully wrapped packages, things too fragile to be transported on the larger cargo rail cars. A small smirk sneaked on to her face.

"Don't even think about it. You're not getting out of your seat until we reach Rhiodeja." I gave her a shove toward the stairs into the car.

"Good, I'll have your attention the whole ride. I'm sure your friend isn't going to give me the time of day."

She hopped up the steps and I followed her, wincing as my feet left the ground and I became surrounded by dead wood and metal. Otsoa had found us seats by a window. The panes opened inward like shutters. He had pulled them in and latched them there. I slid into the bench seat facing him and Drinn sat down beside me. Otsoa was intent on a sheet of paper on the table between us, but the pen in his hand was slack.

"Waiting on a message?" I asked him. There was some writing on the sheet already, some in his scratchy hand, some in a flowing script.

"Yes, I was waiting to hear from Glenn. I found some of these in the bag Negri gave me, and since you were asking him about the Ways I thought it would be a faster way for him to let us know about it."

"That's not Glenn's handwriting," I said, nodding to the clearly feminine swirls.

He blushed. "Well, I figured it wouldn't hurt to let Josie have a sheet too." The messages on it were short. Message paper was not cheap. But it would allow them to say at least one cute thing to each other a day.

I let one corner of my mouth twitch up. "And that plate you got for her. That must have set you back a bit."

He got a wistful smile on his face and started fingering a woven bracelet on his left arm. I hadn't noticed it before, but it looked like a unity bracelet. They were an old human custom, handwoven and gifted to a person's intended. He wasn't the only one researching customs.

"She's more than worth it," he said.

"Of course she is," I said. "But it's not like Wardens make that much."

"I've been saving," he said. "Besides, with what Roya paid us last time, well, it took care of that. Not enough to deal with my family, but there's not enough money in the world for that."

"Yah, family can be such a pain," Drinn said. She was scribbling on the message paper.

"Stop that," I said, snatching it away.

"Apparently he can afford more," she said. She smirked at Otsoa then pointed at me. "Are you still always broke? Never mattered how much money we made, you always needed more."

"I require some very pricey materials to do what I do." I slapped the page back on the table.

"You could learn to improvise, like I do." Otsoa patted his new pack. "I mean, if I bought top-of-the-line things like this all the time, I'd be broke too."

Drinn huffed. "No use trying to get her to do that. Only the best for this one. To be fair, she does have the best illusion I've ever seen."

She had the sense to keep her voice down as she said it, but Otsoa raised his eyebrows and looked at me. I just rolled my eyes.

"You did know she's always disguised, right?" Drinn said, leaning toward him. "I mean, I know it's legal and all, but she's so mysterious about it. What's your guess? I'm thinking she has terrible scars from something, like a fire or a mishap making a potion."

"Nah, she's just vain. It's a bard thing." Otsoa leaned back. Drinn laughed loud and long.

I glared at Otsoa, and just managed to keep from kicking him. "I'd really rather we didn't talk about that." I looked down and squeezed my hands together. They could press the issue, and Drinn seemed to be in the mood to pester me. Otsoa was staring at Drinn in cold silence, almost daring her to keep going. Thankfully my brother started sending a message, the sound of a quill scratching on paper as words appeared on the page. I snatched it up from the table before Drinn could get a hold of it. She wouldn't understand what it was about anyway, but the less details she saw, the better.

Found Way. Ends 1 day south of North Tower. Made before tower fell. Starts in Solis. Could not connect from here.

Parts of the message went through Drinn's scribbles, but I was able to read it, and wrote back a quick thanks.

"Good news?" Otsoa asked.

"Yes, great news. We have a Way north. We'll just have to find an excuse into the Temple of Solis in Rhiodeja," I answered, tucking the paper away.

"They still have any temples to the old gods there?" Otsoa said.

"Never been to Rhio, have you?" Drinn put her feet up in the bench beside Otsoa. "They have temples to most of the old gods still. Something to do with one of their many theories on magic." She tilted her head at him. "I thought you were a wizard."

"I am. I'm just not a superstitious wizard."

The rail car jerked into motion and started rolling toward Rhiodeja.

Chapter Six

The rail car was hot and stuffy. Someone at the other end was smoking a pipe that wafted a heavy sweet scent when there was no breeze. I hung my head out of the window, drawn to the cool air pushing past us, but that attracted too many looks from the other passengers. So I settled for propping my arm against the rattling window pane, rested my head on my arm, and watched the flat, grassy countryside roll by. It was only for a few hours, I thought, and tried to get some rest. I had a feeling most of our work in Rhiodeja would be taking place at night.

Drinn dozed most of the ride. Otsoa kept fiddling with a long piece of paper that he kept folded up like an accordion. He flipped through the folds to different sections, made a note, flipped to another section, and repeated the process. One of many reasons I had never become a wizard, too much homework.

The railway followed along the path of the aqueduct that stretched from the source of the Lumina River somewhere in the Suderburgs out to Cyfar. A dark blue-green moss and a purplish vine clung to the shaded undersides of the wet stones. The builders of the railway had taken advantage of the stonework of the aqueducts. The rails formed bridges between the pillars, so we rumbled over valleys rather than wasting the horses pulling us up and down the hills. It was all rolling farmland between Cyfar and the Lumina River, dotted here and there with small towns. It reminded me too much of home. I turned away from the window and closed my eyes, pretending to take a nap the rest of the way, while keeping an eye on Drinn.

A sharp turn jostled us all to attention, and the Lumina river came into view on our side of the car, with Rhiodeja spread out on the far bank. Above the silvery waters, the city towered like a group of pale giants gathering together at the river to bathe. Multiple towers, some half the size of all of Cyfar, stretching to ten or more levels, crowded the bank of the river. Thin walkways or stone bridges hung between them. The tallest towers framed the central water screw of the city, but others had their own water systems, including waterfalls and waterwheels. The overall impression reminded me of a child's toy.

The railway car slowed as we approached the station. Drinn stretched and yawned like a cat. Otsoa wrapped his new kit up tight and slipped the paper he had been writing on into a pouch at his waist. I pulled my pack up onto the seat and started gathering my papers, making sure I had everything I would need to get through customs.

The rail car fell into shadow, rolling into the customs building, a tall wooden structure with a canvas roof that billowed in the breeze. We jolted to a stop and were surrounded by lines of people unloading the second car and greeting passengers as they stepped down. We filed out and were shepherded straight into the customs line. It was long but was moving at a good pace.

"They are going to take me aside," I said to Otsoa. "You guys can go ahead, and I'll catch up."

"We can meet up at that spot in the main plaza, with that stupid goat on the sign—" Drinn elbowed Otsoa. "You'll love it."

Otsoa grunted and stepped away from her. "You sure you don't want us to stay with you? Just in case?"

I shook my head. "It's better I go through alone. You really will like that goat place. Really good coffee. I'll be fine." He didn't look convinced, but he didn't argue.

We made it to the front of the line and presented our packs and our licenses, as well as a paper proclaiming us as Wardens on an active job. The papers were signed in Roya's name, though they had been written up by Negri. I had one more card than Otsoa and Drinn did, and as I passed it over, the clerk sighed and waved me out of the line.

"Wait over there," he said. He tucked a long strand of dark hair behind his pointed ear. "Someone will be by in a moment." I waved to my companions and stepped over to a small roped-off section of the long room. I counted twenty people getting through customs before a large woman approached me and told me to follow her. She was tall, broad shouldered, and had her golden-brown hair tied up in a severe bun. I hoped she was in a good mood. She wasn't the kind I wanted to upset.

She led me to a stall at the far end of the building, not sheltered by the canvas roof, and had me stand in the full sunlight. Then she raised her hand and made a circling motion, so I turned around slowly.

"You're very good," she said, then looked down at my illusion license. I rarely had to use it, as I didn't travel far from Cyfar unless it was to a tower.

The only places that had full customs checks were the bridge to Rhiodeja, and the road into Alte. Legally I had to prove I was allowed to wear an illusion as part of my job, and legally they had to let me. Mostly the law was to protect some very powerful, very old elves who liked to pretend they still looked fresh as spring. But it also allowed Wardens to travel under cover with few consequences.

"Thanks."

She cleared her throat. "Will you swear that you are wearing this illusion for the purposes of working as a Warden only, and that you are not hiding anything that could be harmful or destructive to the people of Rhiodeja." She recited it with little inflection, bored from how many times she must have had to repeat it.

I looked her in the eyes and nodded. "I swear."

"Are you planning to stay long?"

"No, two days at the most."

"Any violation of your oath will result in the revoking of your license, both for illusion and as a Warden, and you will be held for further questioning."

"Understood." I folded my hands and waited.

She punched a hole in my card with a small device and handed it back to me. She took the tiny bit of paper that had been punched out of my card and put it into a small envelope. "All right, on your way."

"Thank you." I skittered around her and hurried out of the building. It was the least grueling customs check I had ever been through, and it left me uneasy and paranoid, as though they meant to be watching me closely while I was there.

#

I never could figure out what the name of the food stand was, but it still had the faded sign of a goat hanging over the window. It was little more than a space in the wall with a counter under a wide window for ordering, and a row of mud ovens along one side that was constantly baking meat and vegetables. The other wall was taken up with a long counter where the owners prepared food and coffee. Patrons would come up to the window, order something, and the order would echo through the small space for a few minutes in a language that was a strange mixture of halfling and old human. Eventually the flatbread-wrapped fare was delivered to the window, payment was collected, and the customer could take a seat on one of the benches spaced out along the walkway to enjoy their meal.

I pushed through the crowds and found Drinn and Otsoa munching their wraps down the street, sitting on a low wall since all the benches were full. Without a pause in eating, Otsoa held one up for me. Drinn passed me a coffee. Her mouth was full as well, and she had another of the wraps balanced on her leg. I took a bite through the thick, doughy wrap, happy to find only spicy vegetables and cheese inside rather than the greasy-looking meat sticking out of Drinn's.

"Everything go alright?" Otsoa asked. He wiped his chin with a handkerchief. We had to raise our voices over the sound of the waterwheel in the garden behind us.

"Yes, all set." I watched Drinn devour her first meal and start on the next. "All that vanishing make you extra hungry?"

"Oh, look at you making deductions," she said, her mouth half full. She pointed her food at Otsoa. "Watch out, she's gunning for your job."

"So where to next?" Otsoa wiped his hands and tucked his handkerchief away. "Negri said we had rooms at The Heights?"

"Right." I took a look around, getting a feel for the city again. It had been a long time since I'd been here, and many of the shops in this area, what they called the Welcome Plaza, had changed. Three wide stone-paved streets led out from the center, one straight west into the tallest cluster of buildings, one southwest that stepped up in elevation as the ground rose into broad hills, and one northwest into a less crowded section hung with bright, many-colored banners.

"It's probably south," Drinn said, finishing her food and wiping her hands on her trousers. I noticed sticking out from her tight black overtunic. It was a Warden's badge, not worn as prominently as Otsoa's or mine. Negri must have given it to her. I knew she would never have chosen to earn one.

"I think he said Draper Street?" Otsoa was looking around as well, but in a distracted way, like he couldn't decide what to focus on. His hometown, Rheste, was a fair-sized city, as was Cyfar. But Rhiodeja was as large as both of them combined. The streets were crowded with people hurrying to their destinations or salesmen competing for the attention of the hurrying crowd. Horses and carriages clomped by, taking newcomers deeper into the city. The crash of rushing water surrounded the plaza.

"South then," Drinn said, heading down that street. "The cushy ride is over."

"I was surprised that we got as much as we did on top of the promise of payment after." I waved them both on to a side street that paralleled the main market road we were on, a much quieter and shadier street lined with private offices rather than shops. "It won't be any worse than camping out on the road."

Drinn tsked with her tongue. "Where do you usually stay when you're in town?"

"I've only stayed in the barracks." I couldn't afford to splurge on even the cheaper places in this city. Wardens could stay in the barracks, where they housed new trainees, for free.

"Oh, well, you probably won't mind then," she said with a shrug.

Otsoa seemed a little more at ease here, no longer overwhelmed by the crowds. There were still steady streams of people along the street, but there were far fewer vendors. Several blocks around us had multiple levels, but they weren't constructed like those around the plaza with rushing falls of water or massive moving machinery.

Most of the buildings here spanned several blocks, with archways built over the streets. They weren't as tall as they were in the center of the city, but still some stretched more than five or six levels up. Rather than all the levels being the same size, here they varied depending on the function of the building or the aesthetic of the builder. Some had thin spires sticking up from wide lower levels; others alternated full block levels with smaller ones. All were open to the air for the most part, though I did spot a few with panes of glass over more secure areas to afford a view for the residents. Sheet glass was still tricky to make, and most of it was reserved for use in the towers or the churches.

The street names were marked out by plaques on the corners of the buildings, but only the elvish names were immediately visible. I veered closer to one as we walked and saw the name repeated in human, dwarvish, and halfling in much smaller letters underneath, though I doubted a halfling would be tall enough to read the plaque so close. We were already in the guild district, the last street marked as Brewer. After several more blocks we found the right street, and not long after that we were standing in front of drab block of stone with no windows that looked stunted compared to the soaring buildings around it. The plaque over the door read The Heights in blocky elvish letters.

There was nothing remarkable about the place. It was clean, and the elf behind the desk barely looked at us as we retrieved our keys and headed up to our rooms. The levels were not set as far apart as they were in Cyfar, though there were still a lot of stairs before we reached the fourth floor and were able to set down our packs. The room wasn't much bigger than a room in the barracks, though the beds weren't bunks and each was fitted with its own set of curtains for privacy. We also had a round table and a few chairs in one corner.

Drinn dropped her bag, tucked the Warden's badge under her tunic, then pulled a thin roll of fabric out of her pack and tucked it into a pocket on her trousers.

"I'll be back soon. Don't go for dinner without me," she said.

"Where are you going?" Otsoa had set his new bag on the table and stepped in front of the door to keep her from leaving.

"To case the Temple of Solis, of course." She tried to reach around him for the door.

"Not without us you aren't." He raised his hand to her shoulder and pushed her back gently so she was a few feet away from the doorknob.

She looked amused. "I'll take Glade with me, if you insist. But you'll be a bit too . . . Obvious."

Otsoa shook his head. "We all go, or no one does. And why insist on treating this like we're breaking in? It's a temple, right? Isn't it open to worshipers?"

Drinn sighed, turned, and flopped down on the bed she had claimed. "Some of them are and some of them aren't. I just thought we could benefit from a quick look over so we knew what we were dealing with. But if you want to just barge in there and make an offering to the sun in exchange for snooping through the building, be my guest."

Otsoa shot me a pained look and waved urgently at Drinn. I rolled my eyes and moved to the head of Drinn's bed so I could peer down at her. She was trying to keep from grinning up at me.

"We're all going together," I said. "We're just taking a look. Right?"

"Right. Fine." Drinn sat up and straightened her tunic. "Let's go take a look."

WALTZ OF THE GOBLINS

Chapter Seven

I hated to admit it, but the city of Rhiodeja was a marvel. Not every building was amazing, but almost all of them featured some feat of engineering or even magical installments designed to dazzle or draw the eye. As we drew closer to the Temple Plaza, the buildings became taller with stranger and more daring structures. One of the buildings looked like it had a giant egg balanced on top of a tall spire.

We followed the walkway between two massive pillars on to a circular plaza paved with large stones in a kaleidoscope of colors. Several more sets of pillars repeated at each entrance to the plaza. We stepped out on to a set of vibrant blue stones that transitioned to green to the left and purple to the right. Blue meant we were nearest the Temple of Medite, the old goddess of the sea. As we came around the pillar it came into view, a large pool of water nearly as blue as the stones with delicate arches placed around the edges made of glistening pearl. Stepping-stones lead from the front gate to a large round structure that rose from the middle of the pool, wide enough to house a few hundred worshipers.

As we transitioned to green, we passed what used to be Ria's Grove. There were no trees there now. In fact, I couldn't remember seeing a tree since we had arrived. Instead, it was a wide green lawn with multiple containers filled with dirt and overflowing with crop plants of all kinds: beans, squashes, wheat, all tall and green. There were quite a few visitors milling around the planters, watering things or examining the leaves for insects. I shivered, not used to anyone still openly worshiping the old gods. Ria, considered to be the mother of all things Wild, was one of the first to fall out of favor centuries ago. There was nothing Wild about this 'grove' though, just sad confined plants cultivated to do what was needed instead of allowed to grow how they wished.

Next the stones turned to gleaming white, and I edged my way closer to the outer edges of the crowd toward the Temple of Mosine.

"Mind if I stop in here? I won't be too long." I asked. The temple here looked more like a theater, its large double doors thrown open wide. "I haven't been to one in a while."

"What happens if you're unfaithful, eh?" Drinn tapped her knuckles on the gray stone of the building. "Will she take away her favor? Leave you singing drowsy drinking songs in some shack of an inn somewhere?"

"I don't know. I haven't let it go longer than a year." Not that Drinn didn't know that. She had teased me about it when we'd worked together.

Otsoa gave me a strange look. "Are you serious?"

I shrugged. "When I became an official bard, they told me not to let it go more than a year between temple visits. It's not like it's very taxing. Just have to play a song. I'll be right back out."

"I hope so," Otsoa said. "We'll wait for you in the Temple of Solis. Looks like there's a line anyway." He was right, there was a queue around the next temple over.

"Thanks." I watched them take their place at the end of the line and ducked inside.

The first notes I heard coming from the Temple of Mosine were discordant and sour, and I thought it was because all the other noise from the plaza was interfering. But as I passed through the lobby and stepped into the main auditorium, I realized that no one was playing music in the temple. There were just several different people, sitting in different parts of the large room, messing around with various instruments. I stopped in the doorway and stared, waiting to see if they were only tuning or taking a break between songs.

Mosine was one of the few old gods, along with Petos, who were still universally and openly worshiped. A temple to Petos might be full of noise like this, various craftsmen banging on anvils or hammering nails or whatever, but Mosine's temple usually rang with beautiful music. Instead, it sounded like a group of children torturing animals.

"What is going on here?" I asked as an attendant came over to greet me. He was dressed in a short tunic and very tight pants, all in white, with silver embroidery over every inch of it. A floppy hat with a silver feather covered his pale hair. Even his eyes were a pale, silvery blue.

"Greetings." He looked embarrassed, glancing over his shoulder at the would-be musicians. "We are in the middle of a study hour. The city has requested we accommodate those who are investigating the magic of the old ones."

I raised an eyebrow and looked over the people more closely. They would play a note or strike a drum, make a few notes, adjust something on the instrument, and then try again.

"But we know how Mosine and Petos give their magic," I said, then added on as an explanation, "I'm a bard."

"Welcome, honored one." He bobbed a short bow. "We know a way"—the young elf sighed—"a way that only works at the whim of the old ones. They are trying to find the secret to gaining the magic on their own terms." He shook his head at them.

"They want to make Artisans into Spellcasters?" Most people believed the old gods were the source of the magic Artisans used, and unlike spellcasting wizards who went to years of university to learn the technique behind their magic, Artisans studied under a mentor. When they had learned their art well enough, they would bring a masterwork to Mosine or Petos and ask for their blessing. If they found favor, everything they made after could be imbued with magic.

At least, those of us who could work magic that way figured that was what happened. Bringing a masterwork to a temple involved a massive party and falling asleep in the temple at the end of it. The magic would be there in the morning, or it wouldn't. There was no objective information about why it happened, only that the magic would come.

The man shrugged. "I am sorry, I am sure you had hoped to offer a song."

"Have you tried to show them?" The person closest to me had a guitar, and was tightening a string so harshly it snapped, stinging her hand. It made me cringe.

"I am sorry, I am only an attendant here, still an apprentice. I have not been honored as you." Judging from his voice I imagined he would be a sweet high tenor, though music was not the only art honored by Mosine.

"What are you studying?" I asked.

He smiled and gestured to his clothes. "Embroidery and weaving. I am getting close to my day, but my master says I need to learn some balance." He slumped down a little and ran a hand over his tunic. "I do tend to go overboard, I will admit."

"It's hard to hold back when you finally get good at something," I said. "I think I played the same song for three days straight when I finally got it right. Drove my mistress nuts."

His smile widened, and he looked around, then leaned closer and lowered his voice. "You know, we have a Lutherian guitar in the back, if you'd like to give a demonstration."

"Really? You'd let me—" I stopped myself and looked around. As much as I wanted to play a magic instrument, a truly magical instrument created whole by an Artisan, it wouldn't get through to this crowd. "I'm sure they've heard a hundred magical songs, seen a hundred works of real art. What they want is to be a part of it." I chewed my lower lip, and then smiled at him. "Would you mind if I tried something else?"

"Please," he said, clasping his hands in a begging gesture. "Anything would be a relief."

I nodded, then headed for the stage at the center of the room. Built like a theater-in-the-round: the stage sunk into the ground at the middle, and the circles of seats around it built up onto tiers that stepped up to ground level. When I reached the center, I heard my footsteps echo around me, and sighed in happiness at the perfection of the acoustics in the room. When I clapped my hands and cleared my throat, everyone heard it loud and clear.

"All right, everyone, if I may have a moment of your time." I didn't want to waste this opportunity, so I started with magic right away, instilling my voice with enough of it to make them stop what they were doing and pay attention. "I would like to take part in your experiments today, if you will allow me that pleasure, and see if we are able to help you see a glimmer of the magic Mosine may grant to those she favors."

There was a quiet murmur from the crowd that sounded mostly positive. I waved for them to come closer and arranged them around me in the first row of seats: strings to my left, woodwinds to the right, and percussion in front. I was a little sad no one had brought a horn, but I guessed that would have been too loud for the others to conduct their tests.

"I understand why you have chosen music as the best way to study the magic of the arts," I said, settling into my speech. "It is the most mathematical and elegant of them, and easiest to measure. But there is a large part that is not so easy to describe, something that can only be felt. And I would like you to help me in this study, so you know what else to include in your experiments." I walked to the drummer first. He had a simple frame drum that he had been striking with a padded mallet. "Don't use that," I said, taking the mallet from him. "Just use your hand. Strike a beat."

The man began a decent rhythm, steady, but quick enough to not be plodding. I smiled and moved to the strings next. There were three players, one with a guitar and two with viols. "Play a G for me?" I asked each of them in turn. "Tune to her," I said, pointing to the one closest to a true G, and they quickly obliged, and were soon droning out the same note. I kept one droning, then coaxed the other into hopping back and forth between that note and the fifth above it. I started the guitarist on arpeggios, and she kept in time fairly well. By the time I reached the woodwinds, two flutists—who looked like they may be brothers—were already eager to jump in, so I simply held out my hands and motioned for them to start. They wove a melody together over the rest of the music that flowed and bubbled like a stream.

I stepped back to the center of the room and just listened, letting the music wash over me and take my mind where it wanted to go. This was not the forced abundance of feeling that the Wild Song of Summer pushed into those who heard it, but a gentle sweeping away, like laying back in a slow-moving river and floating off. I began to hum, softly so I could be sure I was in the right key, and then louder as I found the notes. I never sang any words, I just let the feelings and impressions from the musicians around me guide my thoughts, letting it create images and call memories into my mind. Then I sang back to them what they gave me, throwing all their thoughts and feelings back at them while harmonizing with the wandering flutes.

The music swelled, becoming a theme that rose and fell, and the room around us began to hum with the sound. Lights danced over our heads and through our hands and spun around the attendant in colored swirls. The image of a bubbling brook formed down the center of the room, so clear I wanted to reach out and touch it, but I knew that would ruin the illusion. The water burbled around the room and then splashed against the main shrine in an explosion of light as the song ended.

The musicians were breathless, and they smiled up at me with the shining eyes of children watching their first fireworks. I applauded them.

"That friends, is magic. Magic doesn't come because you tell it to. Magic bubbles up from inside until it spills out in all directions. You just have to learn how to let it."

#

I hopped into line with Drinn and Otsoa, drawing a few annoyed glances from the people behind them. It had moved quite a bit since they had arrived, and they were getting close to the door. The walk was paved with bright yellow stones flecked with real gold. The Temple of Solis rose like a sunrise frozen in metal, long spiked rays fanning out from a massive dome. The door was round as well and carved all around with old elvish characters.

As we stepped inside, Drinn held her hand over her eyes and tried to look around. "I think it's brighter in here than it was outside."

"It's the mirrors," Otsoa said. He was squinting up at the dome. I looked up as well and saw that it wasn't solid metal but a mesh open to the sky, made of a thousand tiny mirrors placed at every possible angle. So long as the sun was up, there would be sunlight inside the temple, and I wondered if it reflected enough starlight at night to keep it bright without candles or lamps.

I squinted around the main hall, which took up most of the dome. There was only a small section walled off in the back to create offices for the attendants of the temple. There was a long line, but none of the people seemed interested in the temple itself. Any of the implements that would have been used for worshiping Solis—a statue of the god or any of the large, mirrored contraptions used to watch the sun—had been removed. The line we were in was leading into the back office.

"So, what are we waiting in line for?" I said aside to Otsoa and Drinn.

Otsoa shrugged, then turned and tapped the shoulder of the person in front of us. "Pardon me, but what are you waiting in line for?"

The dark-skinned elf turned around, took one look at our group, spat out a short sharp laugh, and turned his back on us again.

"Well, that was helpful," Drinn said. "As if we didn't already stick out as tourists." She looked up and down the line but craned her neck and stretched herself up as though she were only getting a good look at the building, trying to play into our new tourist cover. "There's at least three not guarding their bags very well."

"Before we resort to petty theft . . ." I said, "let's try asking one more time." She pouted at me but got back into line. A pair of attendants decked in golden robes were making their way down the line, filling out papers as they went.

Drinn sighed, then shrugged, then folded her arms and slumped against the wall and moved sluggishly as the line inched forward. Eventually the attendants reached us.

"Names?" the older one asked, a long mustache quivering over his lip as he spoke. The younger one poised a pen over her sheaf of pages.

"Uh, Otsoa Stranero," Otsoa said. The young woman scratched it down, and the older one looked at me expectantly.

"Actually, we weren't really here for . . . whatever this is." I waved my hand at the line. "We were just hoping to take a tour." The people in line around us stopped their conversations to turn and glare at me.

The attendant's eyebrows furrowed, but he otherwise remained bored. "No one is allowed to roam the temple, as it would create an unfair advantage for the competition. And if you are not here for this," he waved at the line. "then I suggest you leave."

"Competition?" Otsoa asked, a little too eagerly. Drinn was already inching away from the line and nodding her head toward the door.

"You are clearly from very far out of town." The attendant looked Otsoa over. "So I will allow my assistant to explain." He took the sheaf of pages and pen from his attendant and continued to the next person in line. The attendant blinked at us a few times, her hands still raised as though holding her notes.

"So, what's this competition?" Otsoa asked.

The attendant sighed. "The Golden Sun Competition was started fifty years ago by High Elder Marvello," she said as though she had repeated it a hundred times today already, "to commemorate the first spell cast outside of Ventor's power that created flame. No one has been able to imitate the spell since, and Marvello has promised great riches as well as a home in the Bright Gardens of Rhiodeja to anyone who is able to cast such a spell."

Otsoa's eyes sparkled, and he turned aside, already doing calculations for a spell that would win the contest. I shook my head and thanked the attendant, then tugged at Otsoa's sleeve.

"No," I said. He ignored me. "No," I said louder. He frowned at me but mumbled something that sounded like agreement. I turned back to the attendant. "Is there something we can sign that promises we won't enter the competition? We really just want to see the building."

"I'm, uh, not really sure." I had caught her off guard. "I mean, why else would you want to see the building?"

"It is really pretty," I said, looking up at the mirrors. "I'm curious about the architecture."

"I suppose I can ask. Wait in line, and I'll be back." She bowed and hurried after the other attendant, not at all sounding like she thought she would find us an answer. I turned to see if Drinn also thought she was planning to ignore us, only to find that Drinn was gone.

\#

We hopped out of line and hurried out the doors, though I was sure we wouldn't catch sight of Drinn anywhere.

"Please tell me you got something from her," Otsoa asked. He was weaving and ducking through the crowd in the temple plaza with his feline grace, barely brushing the people around us. I on the other hand had to apologize every other moment as I knocked people's elbows or blocked their path. He stopped in a quiet, dark archway that the crowd was avoiding.

"Do you usually take hair or something from everyone you go out on a job with? Or just the ones you don't trust?" I started rooting through the pouch at my belt, and he frowned at me.

"Actually, if we're going into dangerous territory where we might all be separated, yes, I do."

"Well, that's not creepy at all."

"It's very convenient. If you lose part of your party or they get captured, you can find out exactly where they are." He looked steadily back at me when I raised my eyebrow. "It's not creepy if you get their permission."

I huffed and pulled out a small lock of Drinn's hair. I wondered if he had some part of me tucked away in one of his pouches.

"Does she know you have that?" he asked, nodding at the hair.

"No," I said handing it over. "But I thought it would be a good idea to get something while she was sleeping. In case she did something like this."

"I guess they are waiting to see if we succeed." He took the hair and pulled out a few bottles from his new pack. The purple powder he shook over the hair was finely ground and shimmered, even in the shade. While he whispered a spell over the hair, I looked around at where we had stopped. An archway of polished obsidian stretched high above us into a multi-spired tower. The plaza flagstones were black as well, and though the crowd was thick everywhere else, no one wanted to step on the black stones. I tried to peer into the darkness beneath the arches. There were no doors, only a deep shadow that seemed to suck the heat out of the air around us.

"You about done?" I turned back to him, hoping that I kept my nerves from twisting my face.

He smirked at me, looped a string around the lock of hair and let it dangle from his hand. It glowed violet but remained hanging straight down. The smirk turned into a twisted frown.

"Is it not working?" I wanted to turn my back on the cold shadows in the archway. I thought I could see strange shapes on the edges, like fingers reaching out of the darkness. But the idea of turning my back on the emptiness behind me sent chills down my spine.

"It's working. It's just not detecting her. She can't have gotten that far away yet." He scooped the hair back up into his hand. Then he looked around at the temple above us. "I really doubt this could be affecting things. I mean, it doesn't even look like anyone is here. Maybe one of the other temples, where they are messing around with magic, but . . ."

"This isn't the sort of magic they would want to be messing with."

"You won't even say his name, will you?" Otsoa laughed, moved into the darker shadows, and waved his arms around. "Hello Mori! Anyone home?"

"Stop it," I hissed at him. "Stop messing around in there, all right?" I waved for him to get out of the hall.

He just laughed again and waved jauntily into the darkness of the temple of the god of death. I turned and walked back into the plaza and he hurried to keep up with me. "Sorry, I forgot you kinda still believe in these things." He vaguely waved around at the temples.

"My magic comes from somewhere."

"Surely. Same place as mine."

"From calculations and finely made lenses?" I shook my head and chuckled. "I don't know anything about those things."

He started to argue, then a surprised look flashed over his face, and he opened his hand. The small tuft of hair darted out and started pulling to the left, stretching the string taut. We darted left into a side alley and hurried along, dodging around barrels and hopping over clogged drains. We ended up on a shady residential street. Strings of fabric leaves hung between the buildings.

57

The hair pulled more to the left and then fell limp again. Otsoa stuttered out something between an oath and a bleat and shook the string so that the hair bobbled in the air.

"This is ridiculous." I stomped further down the street to the left. "If she has some kind of shielding against it, why isn't it constant? And if she is close enough to detect her, close enough to make it pull that strong, why isn't it still working?"

"Fascinating," Otsoa said. "I wonder what—"

It jumped again, pulling the opposite way up the street and we spun around to follow it. It stayed taut longer this time, leading us three full blocks before it fell slack again. I growled and stood staring at the clump of hair, tapping my foot.

"I've never seen anything like this." Otsoa sounded like he was examining a new kind of insect. "Oh look, there it goes again!" It only pulled slightly this time, to the right of where we were, and fell slack right away.

"This isn't one of your experiments, all right? We need to find her." I tried to snatch the charm out of his hand, but he pulled it away.

"This is just the easiest way to locate someone," he said, amused. "There are other ways. But I need more time and some space to work."

I sighed. "Fine, back to the room then? How much more time? The longer we wait the farther away she gets."

"About an hour. It will be a stronger spell, so even if she were running straight out of the city, she won't be far enough away to escape it." We started walking back to our rooms, watching the hair pull several more times, each in a different direction, before we got there. Whatever she was doing, I hoped Otsoa's magic was stronger.

Chapter Eight

Otsoa pulled the table away from the wall and took down the picture of Ventor the Breaker standing over a broken, fallen tree. I flipped it face down on the table. Then he spent several minutes examining the wall through the lens on his wand, muttering to himself and making notes.

"Actually, I could use your assistance with this one," he said, not looking away from the wall.

"I told you, I don't know anything about spellcasting," I said.

"Right, but you're an artist. Think you could draw a door?" He held out one of the bottles from his kit. It was filled with dark ink.

"Depends. Does it have to be very realistic? I'm not that great with drawing."

"I'm sure you'll do better than me. I can't draw a straight line to save my life." He unfolded his kit on to the table and started pulling out other bottles and vials. "While you do that, I'll get the rest ready."

"So what's the door for?"

"We are going to call her to us. Some people prefer a circle on the ground and such for this spell, but like I said, I was never very good at drawing."

"You can't use a real door?"

"Right. It's not about using an actual portal. It's more about creating something that will call or contain them." He shrugged. "I could use a real door, but then we get into the realm of things like portals. And I don't like to mess with those." He glanced at me sideways but didn't explain further.

I looked at the bottle of ink, then at the wall again. Without a decent brush, hand drawing it was going to be tricky. A quill pen may have worked better but the lines wouldn't be as solid. And I wasn't about to use my fingers.

"Do you have any string and some tacks?" I asked Otsoa. He pulled out a small metal bowl, poured a small amount of oil into it, and set it on fire.

"String yes, tacks no." He nodded to a corner of his bag where a roll of twine peeked out from one of the pockets. I snatched it up, then set to prying a few nails out of the bed frame, the table, anywhere I spotted one that was a little loose. I took a deep breath before tapping them into the smooth, plaster-coated wood of the wall and floor. Roya and Negri had provided the usual insurance against property damage, but I always tried not to abuse it. That was the best way to end up only being able to stay in the dumpiest hotel rooms in any city.

I slid several lengths of twine into the ink bottle. Then I stretched the twine between the nails, making sure it was tight, and snapped the string against the wall, leaving very straight lines between the nails.

"Cheater," Otsoa commented.

"You're just jealous you didn't think of it." I waved my inky fingers at him, then sang a quick cleaning song to clean my hands. The hotel had provided a pen, and I began drawing in a doorknob and keyhole in the proper place on the wall. "Do you want me to draw in a welcome mat too?" I peered down at the marks he had made on the floor.

"No, that's just so we know how far away from the door we should stand." Thin, purple smoke snaked up from the small bowl on the table, and the sharp scent of copper filled the room.

I backed out of the square and looked over my drawing. It wasn't great, very flat and barely shaded. But it was recognizable. "What do you think?" I asked as Otsoa brought the bowl over. It was still flaming, a small blue fire flickering in a regular pattern, not like a real flame should act.

"Like I said, much better than I could have done. The more convincing the drawing, the easier the spell." He began waving the bowl across the 'door,' blowing now and then so the smoke curled against the wall. The barest tint of pale blue began spreading across it stopping at the marks I had made. Once every inch was covered, he took up his wand again and began chanting in old elvish.

There were times when Otsoa's spell chants were a strange mixture of elvish and Old Human words, when he would forget the original spell or felt that the elvish word didn't feel right in that position. He was doing it again now, the words flowing out of him as though he were having a conversation with the door, not like the usual rote memorized chants I had heard from other wizards. With each pass of the wand, though it was still smoky, the door became more tangible. The doorknob began to stick out, a strange shadowy thing that still somehow looked flat, though I could clearly see it protruding if I leaned against the wall. He set down the flaming bowl and dropped half of Drinn's hair into it. A burst of violet shot up, then went out with a cloud of smoke.

His words rose in volume, culminating in a final line of elvish. He reached out, opened the door, and shouted Drinn's name.

Drinn came barreling through the doorway as though she had been running down a hallway toward us and plowed directly into me. I braced myself to slam into the far wall, but we never hit it. Instead, we fell, crashing through rough scratchy things that felt like tree branches. I banged and bumped, and felt blood start to ooze from the scratches on my face and hands. We slammed to the ground—rough, frigid ground that caught at our clothes and stopped our momentum as if caught in a brier bush. Drinn landed on top of me and groaned. I tried to draw in a breath, feeling like a wad of dough slammed on to a table.

#

I pushed Drinn off me, but everything was still dark around us as though night had fallen. There were lighter shapes above us, twisted branches of trees that appeared gray against the dark sky, and a warm golden glow emanated from somewhere. I tried to sit up, and regretted it, pain shooting through my head and my back at the same time. But laying back down felt even worse, like lying on a bed of spikes.

"What happened?" Drinn was in better shape than I was. I had broken her fall, after all.

"You ran away and we needed to bring you back," I said, gasping between my words. "Where are we? Is this where you were hiding?" I had hoped by staying still a few moments that I would start to feel better, but lying on the spiky ground was making me feel worse, like something in the earth was sucking energy out of me. I managed to sit up, pushing through the pain in my back to get away from the draining feeling. The sharp things turned out to be black blades of grass poking up at me. "Well, answer me," I demanded.

Drinn was staring at me, her eyes wide. That strange golden glow was reflected on her face. She started skittering backward, away from me, the sharp grass rasping against her clothes.

"What is wrong with you?" I asked, pulling up onto my knees to see if I could stand.

"Glade? Is that you? What's wrong with you?" Her voice sounded strained, like she was keeping back what she really felt. Even so, she sounded terrified.

"I fell into some weird place, and you landed on me, that's what's wrong with me." I used my frustration to push up to my feet and ignore the wave of dizziness that followed. I looked down at her and she cringed. "Answer me," I growled. She was acting like a coward, but I knew better. Drinn had never feared anything in her life, and if she was pretending to be afraid, she was running a con. I glared at her and waited for an answer.

She slid away a little further before getting to her feet herself and brushed away grayish-white splinters and leaves from the tree. "I don't know what this place is called. I just know I can pop in and out. I can disappear from one place, run through here, and appear at another place. Your wizard pulled me out, so I jumped back in. And brought you with me."

"So you can get us out?" Anger was flushing up into my face, and as it boiled up, the pain in my back and my head faded.

Drinn nodded.

"So do it."

She looked around us. "Well, um, sure, but if I do it here, we will appear in the middle of the street. Don't you think it would be better if we got back up to the room?"

I felt another surge of frustration, and barely kept myself from running over and slapping her for disobeying. Then I shook myself. That was not normal. It didn't even make sense. Drinn was right—it would be a horrible idea to randomly appear in the middle of a busy city street. Drinn was pointing up at something behind me.

I turned to see a shadow of the building we were staying in, not a solid image, as I could see all the walls and rooms within, but no people. The gray tree was growing through the shadow walls as though they weren't there. I looked all around, noticing that there were shadow buildings all around, a ghost of the city, dim in comparison to the strange gray or black trees and brush that grew here. The sky was a black dome over our heads with a dull gray sun. Several more skeletal trees stood around, but this place felt deserted and empty.

"Right. Up we go." Stepping closer to the trunk, I reached up to start climbing, and the tree moved. Part of it swayed away so I couldn't get a hold, and a branch swung down at me. I threw myself out of the way, stumbling back, and nearly knocked into Drinn.

She was still staring at me, her eyes wide, her lips pressed tight together. After a moment she shook her head, then dug into her pocket and handed me a small vial of milky white fluid. "Levitation," she said. "I'll climb up and you can float up. I'll pull you in."

"It doesn't do that to you?" I asked, eying the tree.

"It doesn't do this to me either," she said, waving her hand at me. She stepped around me, a few feet further away than was necessary, and started climbing the tree.

"Do what?" I looked down at myself and choked. My illusion was gone. My skin was glowing amber. Perfect, just perfect. That was going to be a fun discussion. I downed the potion Drinn had given me, feeling the feathery tingle spread out from my stomach. My arms lifted first, then the rest of me grew light as a feather. With just a small jump, I lifted into the air, rising beside the tree, parallel to the shadow wall. I bobbed to a stop a few feet shy of the level our rooms were on. The spell would only let you move for so long before stopping you, a precaution against floating away. Drinn scrambled up the tree, then leaned out on one of the branches to grab hold of me. Even then the tree protested, its branches pulling away from me as I drew closer, and she nearly lost her hold. She pushed me toward the room, and I floated over, stopping a few feet above the shadowy image of the floor, and the tree settled, still keeping its branches away from me, but not moving anymore. She climbed up onto a branch that was also in the room, then looked over at me.

"I have to be touching you when I bring us back in," she said. "But apparently the tree doesn't like it. So I'll have to be quick."

I nodded. She fidgeted with something on her right hand. I hadn't noticed it before, but it looked like she had something stretched across the back of her hand, tied on with straps or chains. After adjusting it, she edged out as far on the branch, then leapt at me. When she hit me there was a flash of light, and we slammed into the wall of the room.

Otsoa shouted and hurried over to us, pulling Drinn away from me roughly, tossing her onto her bed before grabbing me by the shoulders. "Are you all right?"

I looked down at my arms again, but my illusion was restored, dark brown skin as usual. But I could feel everything burning, especially my eyes. "Do I look all right?" I asked. My voice was shaky, and the anger that had been bubbling within dissolved, leaving me nauseous and empty.

"You look scraped up. Your hands are bleeding." He pulled one of them up to examine it more closely. "What happened?"

"I think we are all asking that right now," Drinn drawled from her bed. She was coiled there as though ready to jump away at any moment. "And I think all of us should give an answer."

\#

"I would love to explain what happened," I said. I felt dizzy as the anger drained away, leaving me empty and light-headed. I sank into the closest chair and slumped against the back. "But I have no idea what happened, or what that place was."

"I suppose you don't know why you were glowing either." Drinn remained poised on the bed, one hand near her waist. She kept a dagger or two hidden in her tunic. She stretched her other hand out, looking at the strange thing tied to her hand, but her palm was toward me so I couldn't see it. "Why did your eyes turn fairy green?"

Otsoa raised his eyebrows and looked down at me. "You're still shivering. Was it cold there?"

"Cold isn't the right word." I wrapped my arms around myself and shrunk away from him as he reached to steady my shoulder. "I hated that place. It was so hostile. Everything was dark and sharp and didn't like me."

"You're not making sense," Otsoa said, his expression changing to a worried frown.

Drinn was scowling. "The tree tried to swat you away like a fly. And you hated being there. You were all spit and fire in there. What are you?"

"Me? What about you? Have you been flitting in and out of that place all day? How did you learn to do that? What's that thing strapped to your hand? It's bad enough you've been arrested for stealing. Do you know what they'll do if they learn you've been using magic unlicensed?"

Drinn rolled her eyes, but Otsoa moved between us and held up his hands.

"All right, everyone, calm down please. Let's not start throwing around accusations." He looked pointedly at me when he said it, and I sighed. Too many of us had secrets in this room, and the less we said, the better. It was the same situation I had found myself in when I first worked with Otsoa. If he ever reported that I was part-Wild, I could turn him in for knowing shape-changing magic. And we could hold the same sort of insurance over Drinn's head. We could turn her in for using spells without a license, which would carry a much harsher sentence than the one she was trying to buy off now for theft. To my surprise, Drinn opened up first, without the need for threats.

"I don't know what that place is," she said. "I only know that this takes me there. I can travel through there as much as I want and come back here." She untied the object from her hand and gave it to Otsoa, who placed it on the table where we could both see.

It was leathery, and jagged, like it had been torn from a larger object. The color was hard to pin down, brownish-green and very dark. The surface was wrinkled and worn, and leather straps had been tied to the corners so it could be strapped on. I wanted to poke at it, to examine it close up and see what kind of magic object would allow someone with no training to use it so easily. But Otsoa was right, I was still shivering, and the memory of that dark place, the feeling of rage that had filled me there, the tree reaching down to grab me, turned my stomach. So I stayed cowering in my chair and let Otsoa look it over.

He pulled a set of paper strips from his pack, wet them on his tongue, and touched them to the item. Nothing happened. He frowned, and tried again, this time wetting the papers in water from the basin in the room, but there was still no reaction.

"Well, it's not elven magic." Otsoa tossed the papers into the trash bin by the door. Then he looked at me. "I know you don't want to, but as a magical item . . ."

I frowned and looked up, turning to Drinn. "What do you do to activate it? You don't know any spells, and it didn't look like you were creating anything while using it like an Artisan would."

She shrugged, relaxing back on her bed. Instead of a coiled snake, she looked more like a dog being kept at bay. "I just ask it to let me in."

"Ask it?" I eyed the thing, waiting for it to start inching across the table. It remained in place, a deflated bit of leather. "Does it answer you?"

Drinn laughed. "No. It just lets me in. You're making a much bigger deal out of this than you need to. I've been using it for over a year, and I'm fine. Nothing weird has ever happened to me over there. Nothing like what happened to you. It's just a key of some kind, a magical key to that other place."

"Where did you get it?" Otsoa asked. He opened and clenched his fist a few times as though itching to try it on. I wanted to explain more about that place to him, but not in front of Drinn. But when were we not going to be in front of Drinn? He had just expended a fairly complicated spell to get her here. I had no doubt he had ways of making sure she didn't run off again.

"I traded a part of my soul," Drinn said. "Just a few years of my life mind you, a bargain really, at the black market in Tiangi. Crazy place that. You should visit some time, wizard—you might find some useful stuff."

Otsoa blinked and sputtered, not sure how to respond. He was rarely at a loss for words, and it would have made me smile. But I didn't want to honor Drinn's joke.

"Not funny," I said. "I'll just assume you stole it from somewhere."

She shrugged again. "Well, you know all I'm going to tell you about it. So, on to why your eyes went green."

It was my turn to lose my words. I lowered my head and fidgeted.

"Has that not happened to other people you dragged there with you?" Otsoa asked, seeing that I wasn't coming up with an answer right away.

"I didn't even know I could bring others there with me," she said.

"So how do you know it doesn't always do that?"

"We could test it out," she said, holding her hand out for the thing. "Let me take you there."

"You are not getting this back." He wrapped the leather swatch up in a sheet of thin paper and then tucked it into a pocket on his tunic. "I don't want to keep wasting that much stuff summoning you again. Where were you going?"

"Someone needed to look for a back door to the temple. I mean, it was really cute that you thought we could find this thing the proper way, but—"

"And you were looking for the back door in some other dimension all over the city?" Otsoa interrupted.

Drinn raised her hands, palms up, surrendering. "I guess I'll just take your word that anyone else going into that realm ends up looking Wild. Everyone except for me. And you can take my word that I was just doing my job." She examined her fingernails, which despite the fact that she had always been a climber, digger, lock picker, had always looked perfect. They were painted a shining dark blue. "Did you find the portal at the temple?"

I sighed. "No." I twisted my hands together in my lap. She was going to figure out what I was. It was only a matter of time.

"So we're heading back again after dark?"

"Yes."

She nodded. "We should get some rest then." She turned away from us and buried herself under the covers of her bed.

I looked at Otsoa with what I hoped was an apologetic smile. He just shook his head, then patted my shoulder again. "Are you feeling better?" he asked. "You look less shaken."

I nodded. "Yes, thanks. Do you think I should ask Glenn about that place? The clerics are the only people I've ever heard of using strange forms of transportation like that."

"Couldn't hurt. But then you should get some rest too." He headed to his own bed while I pulled out my paper to send a quick message to Glenn.

Chapter Nine

I woke to hear Drinn unleashing a string of curses in several languages at Otsoa. He was standing at the foot of her bed, a smug smile on his face, his arms folded in a clear expression of his not caring what she yelled at him.

"What's going on now?" I grumbled.

"That flaming idiot did something to me while I was asleep. I do still have some rights. You can't just cast spells on a person without permission." Drinn spat her words out at him, but her venom was countered by her getting tangled up in her blankets. She finally kicked them off her legs, but it threw her off balance, and she had to grab at the mattress to keep from falling out of bed on to the ground.

"What did you do?" I asked him.

"Just a mild binding spell. If she tries to get more than fifteen feet away from me, her legs will freeze." He shrugged. "I thought it wise considering the circumstances."

I rolled my eyes at his casual apathy and peered at Drinn through drowsy eyelids. "You did run."

The anger in Drinn's eyes solidified into something dark. She stared back at me with a harsh glare, making it clear that I was shut out, then got up and started making the bed. Otsoa watched her, then raised an eyebrow and looked at me. I was not awake enough to deal with the situation.

"I'm going to find some coffee," I said, climbing out of bed. "Try not to kill each other before I get back."

"No promises," Otsoa said with a wry grin. Drinn continued to ignore the both of us.

Our room and the hotel hall were lit with dim magic globes, but the lobby had a large window that let in the morning sun. The hotel had some form of coffee available, but normally I would never drink such a weak bathwater brew, but I didn't want to leave the two of them alone for long. I knew they weren't going to get along, and that Drinn would do what she could to get under Otsoa's skin. I had not expected Otsoa to take it on himself to police her actions or keep the leash so tight. Of course, she had tried to run away. I had been expecting it, it was too much a part of who she was. Under normal circumstances Otsoa could have found her easily. But even with this weird device she had, allowing her to get away from us, she would have come back. She was a crooked one, but she'd never quit on a job, even one she had been forced into. If he kept pushing at her, it would only make her want to act out more.

I had to admit though, what was driving me to linger in the lobby sipping gross coffee from a tiny, unhandled clay cup, was the look Drinn had given me. I had seen it before, and it meant trouble. Last time she had walked away from me and a few others who had needed our help. This time she wouldn't be able to get away, and I was worried her only option would be to find some way to hurt us. I made it to the bottom of the terrible cup of coffee, poured another one, and headed back up to the room.

The mood was icy. Drinn had set out her lock picks and was making sure they were all in good condition. Otsoa was preparing different powders and taking notes on what useful spells he would prepare for our evening.

"OK then," I said. I headed to my own pack and checked over my own weapons of choice: my flute, a few potions, and my traveling boots. Carrying a bulky pack with us to sneak into a temple wasn't the best idea, but if we had a chance to slip through the portal tonight, I didn't want to be unprepared.

"All right, look." I clapped my hands together, and Otsoa looked up at me. Drinn just kept arranging her lock picks. "I knew this wasn't going to be fun for either of you, but we have a job to do, and we're stuck doing it with each other. We can make that miserable, or we can make it just another job. That's up to you guys. I can promise you this, if you keep icing each other out, I will play the sappiest, most cheerful song I know and make you both giggle like little girls all the way to the Goblin City."

Otsoa's eyebrows raised, as though he didn't believe I would do it. Drinn snorted, knowing full well I could do it, and had done it once before. She rolled up her kit, stood and turned to Otsoa.

"Please don't put me through that torture, again," she said, and shoved her hand out at him. "I'll play nice if you do."

Otsoa took her hand slowly, looking at up her with a flat smile that was more like a grimace. "Sure. I think I can agree to that. I'll drop the spell when we get out of the city. Sound fair?"

"Sounds fair." They shook hands.

"I'm just getting edgy. It's not really my skill set to go sneaking around a city." Otsoa rubbed his hands against his pants before packing his bag up again. "I don't like being stuck between so many walls either." He sent me a sympathetic glance.

"I'm not exactly looking forward to the trek into the north country," Drinn admitted. "She can tell you how well I do camping."

I tightened the straps on my bag. "Hopefully this portal will get us close enough that it won't be much of a trek, and you can go back to sneaking around the mythical Goblin City."

"You still don't believe it's there, do you?" Drinn huffed.

"Not really. But I'm sure whatever this thing, this super weapon that brought down the North Tower is, it's probably still there. Or at least some evidence of what it was." I waved my hand around to show off how vague our objective was. "Enough to satisfy Negri, I hope."

I was sure it wasn't going to be that easy, but it was good enough for now. The coffee was finally kicking in, and I was thinking more clearly. Glenn had written back. He knew nothing about the dark other plane, but he said he would look into it. He also let me know the songs that would unlock the Way between the Temple of Solis and the North Tower. I wrote back a quick thanks and let him know I owed him one. He wrote back that I owed him a lot more than one, but he also wished us luck.

#

The night was warm and sticky, made worse by the still thick crowds of people in the streets. The crowd thinned as we drew closer to the temple circle and away from the brightly lit taverns and theaters around the city. We strolled quietly through lamplit streets and made it to our destination without attracting any attention.

Darkness muted the colors of the plaza floor, except in small semicircles of light where lanterns cast a glow on to the stones. Everything else was draped in shadow and stillness; the sounds of the city grew muffled, becoming just a buzz in the background.

We kept to the edges of the darkness and walked slow and soft across the plaza to the golden Temple of Solis. This side of the plaza was a little brighter, the colors of all the other lights reflecting off the metallic dome. Drinn motioned for us to follow her around the side of the building, between the Temple of Solis and the one for the goddess of the moon. I kept close watch for any sign of light or life within that one, as the moon was already above us, half full and dull red. Nothing stirred in the whole plaza but the wind and the water around Medite's temple.

A small door recessed into the side of the temple. The frame was bolted into the wall, but there was no clear fastening on the door, no handle or anything on this side of it. Otsoa pulled out his wand to take a closer look, but Drinn waved him away, producing a flat piece of metal the size of her palm from her sleeve. She rubbed it around the frame of the door and it slid open. Otsoa grunted in a mixture of surprise and annoyance.

"What, you think I snuck away from you earlier for the fun of it?" Drinn asked as we stepped into the back rooms of the temple. A long, dark hallway stretched in front of us, lit only by two small windows on the ceiling. Rather than the strange, honeycombed metal that formed the front of the temple, this section was regular stone walls and wooden beams. Three doors lined the hall to our left, and another large metal door took up the wall at the far end.

"How did you know it wouldn't trip an alarm or screech loudly when it opened?" Otsoa asked in a whisper.

"I didn't," Drinn shrugged. "Just like I didn't know there was a back door, or a key to open it, or what time the office usually closes at the end of the day." She made a sour face at him and then crept down the hallway, her hand running lightly along the wall.

"I know you don't like it, but you can trust her a little," I told Otsoa. "This is what she does, and she's good at it."

"Were you good at it too?" he asked. I couldn't see his expression, but I could hear the distaste in his voice.

"Nah, I was just the face of the operation. Usually kept people distracted while she did the real work."

"Looks like we're clear in here," Drinn said, making her way back to us. "No alarms set. So, are you sensing whatever it is we're looking for yet?"

"Not yet," I said. I strode down the hall paying close attention to the doors. The first time I had encountered one of the Ways, it had given me double vision, a strange stretching away feeling when I looked at it, but none of the doors here had that effect. I tried the handle of the farthest door. It was unlocked and opened to a storeroom full of crates and covered chairs.

"There should be an office back here," Drinn said, peeking through the middle door. She frowned and shut it again. "Not even anything worth taking."

Otsoa opened his door. "Looks like I'm the winner. Do I get a prize?" He stepped back and we joined him at the doorway to a large office.

Drinn rubbed her hands together and started into the room, but Otsoa stopped her. He held up a small stone, whispered something, and the stone glowed blue.

"So you don't bang your shin on anything in the dark," he said.

"Nice. Thanks." Drinn took the stone and went into the office. We watched the faint glow wander around the room, and I started to relax. We were fortunate enough to find the place empty, and I hoped that it would go smoothly.

"There's another door on the far side," Drinn said. "I think we can risk some more light, there's no one here." She fiddled with something on the desk and a lantern bloomed to life. The office was lined with bookshelves; a desk took up most of the middle. She kept the lantern low, but we could clearly see piles of paperwork spread out on the desk, copies of the form they had tried to get us to fill out earlier.

While I crossed to the door, still getting no strange feelings, Otsoa looked over the papers on the desk.

"We're running out of places to look," Drinn commented. She tried the door handle, but this one was locked. She clicked her tongue, pulled out her roll of tools and knelt to examine it.

"Well, considering how important they were, the Way is probably part of the sanctuary," I guessed. "Which is what's on the other side of this, right?"

"Should be," Drinn nodded. She took a few tools out and began fiddling with the tumblers.

Otsoa hummed curiously and pulled one of the pages out of the stack on the desk, holding it closer to the lantern. "This one's not half bad," he said mostly to himself.

I shook my head. "Don't mess with those, they were taking it pretty seriously." He still copied down the complex spell pattern on a blank sheet from the desk before putting it back on the pile.

The door clicked, and Drinn swung it open. It creaked the whole way, and Drinn cringed away from it. Light glowed on the other side, which opened into the main dome of the temple. Rather than sunlight, the moonlight was being reflected through the strange ceiling, so the light was reddish and muted, but it was bright enough that we could turn off the lantern in the office.

The main area was divided by a wall several feet from the door, creating another long hallway. This one had several chairs and small desks, probably where the contestants showed off their attempts at imitating the sun god's magic. In the center of the wall was a massive set of metal doors, ornately carved with sun symbols and ancient elven characters. As I studied the carvings, my vision blurred, and I saw three sets of doors overlapping and felt certain they each led somewhere other than the central part of the temple.

"That's it," I said, pointing to the doors.

Drinn shook her head at me. "So, how is it you can see these things and others can't?"

I shrugged. "I honestly have no idea. You'd think Glenn or other clerics would be able to spot them, but he doesn't feel them either." I drew as close to the Way as I dared. They tended to make me queasy. When they were completely closed, I felt more than saw them. The Ways had been used ages ago by clerics in the fight against the Wild, allowing them to travel quickly across the realm almost instantly. Most people had forgotten about them, even leaving them open in some places. This one was closed on both ends. I wondered if I could feel them because Wild people had learned to fear them.

"All right, I'll get started. Keep an eye out." I pulled out my flute and the paper with Glenn's musical notation for the keys to the Ways. The song that opened this side was a simple hymn to Solis, a bright, chipper one. The space before the ornate door blurred and then swirled open into a dark, misty void.

Drinn let out a slow whistle.

"Wait till I get the other side open." The song for the other side was more complicated, and it took me a few tries to get the rhythm right. As the last note echoed through the sanctuary, I paused and watched the slowly spiraling mist.

"Is something supposed to happen?" Drinn asked.

"What's going on?" Otsoa was still in the office room, watching the hallway.

"It's not opening."

"Hang on," he grumbled, shutting the door to the far hallway softly. When he reached the door to the sanctuary, there was a sweeping sound, like the metal door to the alley was sliding open. He froze, his hand on the knob of the open door. Drinn cursed under her breath. I slipped past her in the dim light, scanning through every cover story I knew for something that would buy us enough time to get out.

Otsoa stopped me, moved back to the far door, and whispered something to it. It glowed red and then went back to normal, but whoever was on the other side started shouting.

"Hey, there's someone in there." The door rattled as they tried to open it. "They locked us out!" Several other voices joined them, yelling in alarm.

"We could probably make it out the front," Drinn said. "Glade can make us invisible, and we'd get away clean."

Otsoa guided me back into the sanctuary and locked the second door behind us. We heard the far door bang open just after.

"That lock spell would have stopped anyone but another wizard. No offense, but I doubt your invisibility spell will fare any better against whoever that is. We need to go now. Open the other side." He threw me at the doors, then turned back to the office door. A deep voice was chanting within, and he started to counter it, trying to keep the lock up as long as possible.

"Of course we pick the Watch shift with a wizard," I grumbled, pulling out my flute.

"I don't think they're Watch," Drinn said. She was watching the door warily.

I put the flute to my lips and began the song again, hoping that if I could only play it better, with more feeling, that the other side would suddenly open.

"Otsoa, it's not working. I need you to help."

"Not now." He managed to sneak the words in between lines of his spell.

"I can't do this." I stomped my foot, and then sighed. "I'm sorry, Otsoa." I raised the flute again and began to pull on him through our bond. It was probably the stupidest thing to do when he was in the middle of a spell, but I needed something to force the other side open.

He grunted, groaning like he was trying to lift a very heavy weight. His words stumbled, and the glow on the door began to change from red to blue.

I flew through the song, shoving both my magic and whatever I could pull from Otsoa into the music, and the portal cleared to show grassy hills and moonlight.

"Let's go," I said to Drinn. She gaped at the portal, then at me, but I gave her a shove toward it, and she jumped through.

"You next," Otsoa said over his shoulder. "I have an idea for distracting these guys until you're through."

I jumped through the portal and turned to watch him back away from the door. He turned long enough to make sure he was just before the portal, then focused on the door as it flew open. He finished his spell, and a brilliant light exploded from his hands, not a weapon, just a beam of light that bounced around the room. I couldn't see who had come through the door.

Otsoa jumped backward through the portal, and I played my canceling song. The portal snapped shut, and we were left in the reddish glow of the half-moon in the middle of nowhere.

Chapter Ten

It was cooler in the open. We were close enough to the sea for a constant breeze to wash over us. Massive dark shapes far north, the beginnings of the Spine Mountains, blocked out a vast patch of the starry sky. The dark blots petered down to a rough, spiky shore in the northeast, rows of dead trees reaching up into the night, and the midst of them, was the bumpy blotch of what remained of the North Tower.

Drinn was lying on the ground, rubbing her legs. She narrowed her eyes at Otsoa. "That spell is horrible."

"Sorry." He grumbled a cancellation spell over her to dissolve the tethering, and then added something at the end. She tilted her head and stopped rubbing her legs.

"Thanks." She stood and took in our new surroundings. "Can they follow us through that thing?"

"Not without the songs. Assuming they even know what it was we just did." I shook my head. "Most of the clerics don't even remember those. I doubt the Watch would."

"That was no Watch," Drinn said.

"They had to be Wardens," Otsoa agreed.

"But why were they coming after us?" I tilted my head at Drinn. "Why would they not want us to find this weapon? It destroyed a Warden tower."

"It may not have anything to do with this job. Working for Negri tends to have this kind of collateral hazard. You get used to it."

"You shouldn't have to," I muttered.

"Well, you're the wilderness expert," Drinn said, slapping my back. "What do we do now?"

"Find a place to shelter for the night." I started looking around us for a larger hill or some shrubs.

"Out in the open?" Otsoa asked. He looked skittish. A brief wave of nausea rolled over me, , and I looked at him sharply. He was trying to calm his breathing, but his eyes still flickered around wildly. He was thinking of shifting, and it was pulling on me.

"I'm sorry. Are you all right?" I said, coming up beside him and setting my hand on his arm. I had stopped trying to pull magic from him through the bond, and instead I tightened it, restraining the animal unease shaking his mind. He stilled, and the nausea passed. "I'd rather we spend the night here than closer to the woods. It's better to go through that in daylight. We should be able to reach the tower by noon tomorrow and then follow the map the rest of the way."

"Through the woods? I don't think I like that any better," Otsoa grumbled. "Can't we figure out how to get to the Goblin City from here? Skip the tower altogether?"

"It's not that kind of map," Drinn said.

I spotted a tall hill with a few shrubs along the side that would provide a little shelter from the wind and started for it. They trailed behind me.

"There are kinds of maps?" Otsoa asked.

"Yah. You know, I get that you only throw spells around when you're on a job, but you really should learn at least a little something about what the other team members do." Drinn's voice was growing snippy.

"Right, I'm sure you've been on hundreds of adventures out here, with the Wardens, picking locks and slipping away through dark alleys."

"Don't make me separate you two," I said over my shoulder. "We're going to have to stick close." I checked through the bushes, not that I expected anything Wild in them this far from the forest, but it was wise to be safe this far from any kind of town. The grass was thick in the shelter of the hill and would make a good enough bed for the night. I just hoped the weather held out. We didn't have anything on us to deal with rain or high winds.

"Can we risk a fire?" Drinn asked.

"Yes, I should think so."

Drinn gathered twigs from around the shrubs. I couldn't tell what Otsoa was up to, but he was digging through his pack and trying to read the vials in the moonlight. I pulled out my flute and started counting steps away from the hillside. At twenty-five paces I stopped and turned to my right.

I played a mechanical set of notes, a repeating, not very interesting tune, and began walking a circle around our camp. With each repetition I felt something tighten in my mind, like a thread was tied to my awareness and stretched out behind me along the circle. When I got back to the place where I had started, the loop closed, and for a brief moment, I could sense every movement inside the circle, from a swaying blade of grass to Drinn's striking a flint against a stone. It faded, but if anything new stepped inside the area, I would know it, even if I was dead asleep.

I made my way back to the now growing campfire. Otsoa was mixing something over the flames, and Drinn was trying to snuggle down into the grass under a shrub.

"What are you working on?" I asked him.

"Trying to get us some more shelter." Otsoa paused, blew on to his hands and held them over the fire. "Just need a break in the breeze." He tossed a pinch of whatever powder he had mixed into the air, but it scattered. After a few more times, there was finally a lull in the constant gusting, and the dust settled on to the ground around us. A deep blue twinkling began in the grass, rising from the ground like a fine mist, which solidified into a thin canopy that hovered over our heads and dispersed some of the cold air.

"It should block any rain too," he said.

The canopy was see through, but only faintly, and I didn't like that it reduced our vision. I peeked out from under it and looked northeast again at the leafless forest. It was pretty far off, and I doubted anything would even notice we were here. But this far north, away from any civilization, the Wild may have grown bolder. No one had manned the North Tower in centuries. No one had ever found out what had really happened to it. There had been no survivors.

"Do you want me to add something to the perimeter you put up?" Otsoa asked. "Something more defensive?"

"No, I think that will only draw more attention to us." I took a deep breath and sat down by the fire.

"So what's so strange about that map?" Otsoa asked Drinn.

She scowled at him. "Are you going to make me pull all that out now?"

"You could just tell me about it," Otsoa said. "But I probably won't believe you."

She sighed, grumbled a few choice words under her breath, but stuck her elbow in the dirt, propped her head up on her hand, and reached into her pocket. "It's called a landmark map. At first it only shows you the first landmark you need to reach." She unfolded the map and held it up so he could see it in the firelight. The crude drawing still only showed the ruined tower and a simple shape for the Goblin City separated by an expanse of dead trees. "When we reach the Tower, it will show us a way through the forest to the next landmark."

"What a convoluted way to make a map," Otsoa said. He reached out for it, but Drinn pulled it away.

"Extra layer of security, for very paranoid people. Which I think the goblins would qualify as." Drinn turned the map to look at it. "Though they are still Wild. And since when does anything they do make sense?"

Otsoa peered at the map over the fire with a frown. "Right, well, I hope it's not too long of a trip from there."

"Or at least that it doesn't keep us in the woods for long." I shivered. I had taken people through the Wild before, when necessary, but that was in my forest, the one I was born to.

"You sure you don't want the wizard to whip up something else?" Drinn was watching me closely.

"No, I'll just keep watch for a few hours, and wake Otsoa up at an ungodly hour so I can get some sleep."

He groaned and covered his face with his arms. "Fine, fine. But you're going to have to find a way to make coffee happen in the morning."

I laid down with a groan of my own. I could live without blankets, or a tent, but there would be no coffee for days, and I wasn't sure how I would survive that.

#

I had no dreams at all that night. None that I remembered anyway. It was unusual so soon after Midsummer to not have any haunting images of the Wild claw into my mind in the night, but I decided to be thankful rather than question it. The morning broke sunny but cool, and I only yawned about fifteen times while making breakfast. Otsoa was somehow bright and awake, despite having awakened before dawn to take over the watch. Drinn unfurled like a cat, stretched, and found a patch of sunlight to sit in while she ate the oatcakes I'd made. She was awake, but she didn't seem happy about it. Otsoa tried to engage us in conversation, making comments about the weather or the distance to the tower, but we just glared at him and finished eating in silence. With a snap of his fingers, he dissolved the tent he had formed over us. Drinn spread out the embers and buried the fire, and we started toward the pile of stones that was all that remained of the North Tower.

The distance was deceiving. I had thought we would reach it within a few hours of walking, but it didn't look any closer when we stopped at noon for water. Each rise we topped led to more rolling hills covered in sparse grass and gravel. And always there was the sound of the sea, a distant rhythmic sweeping.

Sadly, the day wasn't too cool for bugs, and now and then we ducked through swarms of gnats or flies hovering in a small valley. They gathered near the scraggly bushes that dotted the hills, but I couldn't guess why. There were hardly any leaves on the bushes and certainly no fruit that would drop off and rot to attract them. They didn't bite, but they got in our eyes, ears, or mouths and were a general nuisance. Drinn gagged more than once and used up some of her water rinsing out her mouth. Though it may have been an excuse to take more frequent breaks, I was happy to let my heavy pack down as well.

We reached the edge of the woods by late afternoon. The trees were even more derelict than the bushes, with no leaves at all, nothing but bones reaching up to a pale sky. Their roots arched out of the cracked ground. No birds cawed or flapped; no rodents scuttled around us. There was only the wind and the sea, which we could see now in glimpses between the twisted trunks.

"I don't like this," Drinn said. She had folded her arms around herself. "Are you, uh, sensing anything?" she asked me, but refused to take her eyes from the trees.

"That's what's worrying me most," I answered. I took a few more cautious steps toward the woods. "I'm not feeling anything. Nothing at all." This area had once been the northernmost reaches of Winter's Forest, that had been burned or chopped back to the south of the Suderburgs. It stretched all the way to the tip of the Spine Mountains far to the north. I should have felt the chill of Winter Wild all over it. But I felt nothing. It was empty.

"That should be a good thing, right?" Otsoa asked. "That means there are no Wild creatures hiding in there?"

"I guess," I said. "Unless they found a new way to hide."

"Good. So, the tower is just there." He pointed to the right. "Let's get there and see what the next leg of this trip looks like." He pressed forward into the trees without hesitation. Drinn and I followed more carefully. It might be that there were no Wild things here, which could be a good thing, or it could mean that something much worse had driven them away.

It was tough going, trying to watch every step so we didn't trip or get tangled in the tree roots, but we reached the tower by dusk. Large stones had fallen from the tower's top and landed in broken heaps around its base, leaving parts of the stairway exposed overhead, though the top was still enclosed. Not a scrap of moss or bit of mushroom was growing on the crumbling gray blocks. The doorway was still mostly intact, its dark archway yawning before us like the throat of some rock giant. Even in its fallen state, it felt larger than the typical towers, the top hidden above the empty branches of the trees.

"Is this close enough, or do we have to go in?" I asked. Drinn was already removing the map. "What's so funny?"

She turned to look at me with a quirked eyebrow. "What?"

"Why were you laughing?"

"I wasn't laughing," she replied, snapping the map open.

"You don't hear that?" I looked around for the source of the dry rasping I had assumed was a laugh. It stopped when I turned my head.

"Hear what?" She looked around as well, but the three of us were alone under the skeletal trees.

"Well, it's gone now," I said with a shake of my head. Otsoa climbed up on one of the stones and disappeared into the rubble. "Don't go too far, I don't plan to stay here long," I shouted after him. He shouted something back that sounded like agreement, but I couldn't hear him clearly.

"It's not working." She lowered the map so I could see. Nothing had changed.

"You're sure it's a segment map? Maybe we're supposed to use it under moonlight or something?" I reached toward it, but she pulled away from me.

"I'm pretty sure. Considering what I had to go through to get it, I know it's authentic, and if it was anything other than a segment map, the previous owner would have figured it out." She glanced at the dark mouth of the tower. "Maybe we have to go inside?"

"Great." I peered around the stone Otsoa had climbed, but there was no sign of him. Climbing over the stone brought me to a mound of rubble between two more massive rocks. They could have fallen in that convenient arrangement, but it was more likely something had placed them that way after they had fallen. Without moss or other growth, it was difficult to judge how long they had been that way. They were worn from years in the wind and rain, so if there had been any markings, they had disappeared. I slogged up the pile of gravel, and found more standing stones, arranged in a circle around a patch of soft earth. Otsoa was crouched in the center of the circle, examining something I could not see.

"What is this?" he asked, without turning to look at me. I moved up beside him. He was looking at a bright yellow flower that stood out vibrantly in the dark earth. "It likes you," he added.

"What?"

"Keep moving around and watch it."

I took a few steps more, and the blossom of the flower turned to follow me. I moved around the whole circle and wherever I went the flower followed, as though I were sunlight.

"The map isn't working. We have to go into the tower." I started back for the graveled entrance.

"Is it Wild? Can you tell?" He stood but kept staring at the flower.

"No. It's not." I reached back to pull at his sleeve. "Come on. Leave it be."

"You're not even a little curious? You don't think it's a clue to what happened here?"

"What happened here is that the Wild stormed the tower, took a chunk out of it, and killed everyone inside." I glanced around the stone circle, then back down at the little flower that seemed to be smiling up at me. "I don't know what did this, but it wasn't the Wild."

"How are you so sure?" he asked as he followed me back over the stones.

"There is nothing Wild here, nothing alive, nothing growing. Whatever that is, it's not real. Not a real flower anyway."

Drinn raised an eyebrow at us as we joined her. "Flowers?"

"It's nothing." I looked again at the ruined opening of the tower, doors long rotted, stones crumbled the way a wave would disintegrate sand. "So, after you." I waved for Otsoa to lead the way.

"Me?" He frowned. "Why do I have to go first? She's the one with the most weapons." He pointed at Drinn.

Drinn rolled her eyes. "You could blast the whole tower to bits, if you're worth anything as a wizard. I think you should go first."

He sighed and looked at me, a question in his glance. I nodded as slightly as I could. If he had to shift while he was in there, I would let him, though I knew it wouldn't be fun trying to explain it to Drinn, and it would probably lead to having to explain what I was. But if there was something in there waiting to attack us, it would also save our lives. He straightened his shoulders, raised his wand in one hand, and readied a vial of something green in the other. Moving toward the door from the side, he took slow, small steps.

The laughter sounded again, still rasping but louder now. Drinn and I jumped, but Otsoa stayed calm, trying to get a glimpse of the source.

Otsoa disappeared into the darkness of the tower's door, then a moment later we saw a faint blue glow outline his shape. He looked around for a few minutes, and then appeared in the doorway again.

"All clear, come on in," he said with a wave.

We shuffled in, Drinn slightly in front of me, a blade in one hand, her other hand slightly behind her and resting on my arm so she could keep track of me. Climbing the winding stairs felt like moving through another world. It was cold and damp, and the darkness reacted strangely to Otsoa's lights as though it were slinking out of the way. As we neared the hole in the wall of the tower, the stairs petered down to a narrow ledge along the inside wall.

Otsoa used some sort of spell to float more than jump, hovering over the gaps in a way that made me hold my breath. Drinn had always been agile and managed to hop from step to tiny stone ledge to step like she was playing hopscotch. I had to be more careful. Though I had a song that could give me increased agility, it was shaky, and I wasn't sure how much noise I wanted to make as we climbed. I took a chance, chanted my song as loud as I dared, and took a few flying jumps. I wavered on the final step, part of it crumbling away under my foot, but Otsoa grabbed my arm, Drinn reached around my waist, and they pulled me to safety.

The top floor was still much like any other tower, a wide circle covered with a solid ceiling and glass windows all around, though the glass was mostly shattered. The central brazier was completely missing, and in its place was a doorway standing free of any wall. The frame held a dark wooden door on large iron hinges that looked like clawed hands dug into the wood. Above the door, a grotesque mask stared down at us, with some kind of shiny dark stones for eyes. The mask was set to look like it was the head of a creature crouched over the doorway.

Drinn pulled out the map and choked, then spread it out with a snap so we could all see it. The tower was still there, but it was faint, and had grown smaller. Instead, there was an image of the door, and spreading out behind it was the larger and more detailed image of the Goblin City. We could count how many towers were along the wall and see outlines of streets and houses.

"We have to go through there?" Ostoa asked, pointing at the door.

"Well, it does look like that's the gate," I said. But I wasn't any happier about it than he sounded.

"Hang on, just wait a moment." Drinn shoved the map back into her sleeve and started examining the doorway, searching around it and feeling along the door frame with practiced, sensitive fingers. Otsoa also waved his wand over it, trying several different spells, each flooding the doorway with a different color light. The door didn't change, move, or react in any way I could see. It didn't look like a Way, either. I felt no stretching and saw no phantom doors multiplying around it.

"I'm not seeing anything," Otsoa said. I shrugged at him, agreeing.

"I don't like it," Drinn said, coming around from the far side of the door.

"There's no tricks or magic on it," I said.

"Exactly. If this is the amazing magical hidden gate to the Goblin City, you'd think you'd have guards, or traps, or something." Drinn shook her head. "It's like it's just for show."

The dry, scraping laugh echoed around us again, louder this time. We all looked up to see the mask laughing. It rose over the door and a body appeared over the edge, unfolding itself from the door frame and creeping sideways so it could leer over us.

Drinn went into an aggressive stance with her knife, and Ostoa pulled a vial of something dark from his pocket, but the longer I stared at the creature, the less afraid I felt.

"Come down from there," I demanded. The others glanced at me in worry, but I held my ground, putting my fists on my hips like an upset mother.

The figure, round and lumpy, with a twisted green-skinned face, jumped down and stood in front of the doorway.

"Who are you?" Otsoa asked the figure, pointing his wand at it in warning.

"Who am I? Who am I? I'm the keeper of this sty. Who are you? And why are you menacing my goblin flower, and trespassing in my goblin tower?" His voice was crackling, but I could tell it was forced, along with whatever accent the small man was trying to imitate. He was also terrible at rhyming.

"We found a goblin," Otsoa said, recovering some of his pride. He still held out his wand but looked less afraid and more excited.

"That's not a goblin," I said, rolling my eyes. "He's wearing a mask. He's just a halfling."

The man in the green leather mask shook his head violently and bounded up to Otsoa. "Don't let her lie to you, more than she already has, the false faced one. She doesn't know. I am a goblin, I am, sure as you're standing here." He tapped the end of Otsoa's wand without a trace of fear and snickered at me. The mask was sewn together from scraps of leather dyed different shades of green and had a twisted smile and long bumpy nose. He was wearing patched together clothes as well, which gave him the lumpy look. Otherwise, so far as I could tell, he was a normal halfling.

Otsoa looked over his shoulder at me, and I shook my head. "Take off the mask then, and let's see."

Drinn leaned in close and whispered to me. "You've seen a goblin before?"

I nodded, but kept my eyes glued to the halfling. He stared back at me.

"I'll take off mine if she takes off hers," he said in a singsong. Something about his eyes was setting off warning bells in the back of my mind. Now that he was closer, I could see that there were domed things over the eyes that gave them the appearance of being solid black, but behind them I could see his own small eyes peering through.

"The thing you have," I started to say to Drinn, and then the halfling ran at me with a growl that was much deeper than I thought could come from something so small. Otsoa got his spell off before he reached me, and the halfling froze a foot away from me, his hands spread out like the claws of an eagle.

I grabbed Drinn's arm and hid behind her, and we both stumbled back a few steps. The halfling was completely frozen by the spell and couldn't talk, but was straining against it, and sounded like he was hissing.

"How long can you hold him?" I asked, my voice squeaking.

"I've had enough of this." Drinn said. She flipped another knife into her free hand and stalked forward. The halfling was so focused on me he didn't react until she had her knife at his throat. She gripped his arm and shook him. "Stop it now, or I'll end you."

The halfing made a strange grunt, and relaxed. His eyes were still on me, but he didn't appear to be straining any longer. Otsoa released the spell, and

Drinn pulled the halfling's arms behind his back, preparing to tie him up. All the halfling did was laugh, and then he and Drinn disappeared.

"What is going on?" Otsoa dropped his arms in frustration.

"Bear with me a minute." I held up my hand and thought over everything again. "I can't believe I'm going to say this, but I think we need to use Drinn's device thing."

Otsoa pulled out the small scrap of leather. "You think it's a piece of a mask, like the one that halfling was wearing?" He made a face, not happy with the jumps in my logic.

"You have a better explanation?"

He held his hands up. "I'm not even trying to explain any of this. Are you sure you want to go back there?"

I took hold of his hand. "No. Let's go."

#

The world melted around me and turned into the dark realm I had been knocked into before, the skeletal trees around us only ghostly shapes under the faint sun. There was no sea breeze, and the sea itself was still as a pond. The feeling that this place was wrong, that I shouldn't be here, rolled over me. Drinn had finished tying up the halfling and was busy trying to gag him when we arrived. He was struggling fiercely, even tied up, and snapping at her hands if she tried to get near his mouth.

I rushed to them, grabbed the halfling and threw him to the ground. The anger that had slowly risen in me before rushed into me this time, especially with such an easy target. I rested a knee on his chest and ripped the mask off his face. His head snapped up and back as the straps of the mask pulled clear and he yelped in pain.

"Where are we?" I growled. "What is this place?" The halfling narrowed his eyes at me, but slowly his face changed to a pleading, hungry look, and he started to whisper something. I leaned down closer to understand the words.

"Please." he said. "Please just a taste."

"Glade," Otsoa sounded worried.

"Just a minute." I turned my face so I was looking directly into his eyes. "Where are we?"

"Glade." Drinn touched my shoulder.

"What?" I snapped my head up to look at her.

She pointed over my shoulder, her eyes wide. I gave the halfling one last shove for good measure, then stood and turned around. We were still inside the ghostly tree line, the contour of the mountains standing out stark against a colorless sky to our right. But before us, as solid as the ground beneath us, was a wall. The wall stretched north and south as far as I could see with no break or change, following the contour of the land.

"Glade, come here." Otsoa waved me over to him. He was on a rise of ground to my left, where he could see over the wall. I climbed up beside him. Beyond the wall were many lower walls, crisscrossing through the space in complex paths. Far west, in the center of it all, stood a tall, twisted castle.

"No," I whined clomping down the hill. "No!" I ran toward the halfling, meaning to kick him in the gut to vent my frustration. "A maze? Are you serious?"

Drinn stood between me and the halfling and stopped my charge. "We need to get you out of here. Let's question him over there." Otsoa came down the hill behind me and put his hand on my shoulder. I clenched my fists and nodded. They were right, but all I could think about was making the halfling pay for the trouble we were faced with. I handed Drinn the mask, and she grabbed the halfling and vanished. Otsoa pulled us through just after.

We emerged in the shadow of the tower. I rushed around the other side of some trees, out of sight of the others, to pace back and forth the best I could over the tangled roots until I calmed down. The feelings had been so much worse this time. The need to hurt someone, anyone, had pulsed through every part of me. It was taking longer to fade away, too. Whatever that place was, the longer I was exposed, the worse it was going to get. But the whole goal of this mission, the Goblin City, was in that place. I felt a tug, a cool, restraining tug, and when I turned to pace back, Otsoa was there.

He tilted his head and looked me over, clinically assessing the situation. "Feeling any better?"

"Getting there."

He took a deep breath, and the pendant at this throat flared gold for a moment. The last bit of rage cooled into a lump of anxiety in my throat. I patted him on the shoulder a few times and took a shaky breath.

"Thanks. I didn't know if it would work for that."

"Neither did I, but I figured it was worth a try."

"What are we going to do? I don't know how to deal with a maze."

"I can handle that. I'm letting her handle the interrogation. I'd rather it be you, but with what just happened—"

"It's fine. She knows where to draw the line." I turned to go back to Drinn, then hesitated. "Did I really, um, when we were over there, I mean could you see—"

"What you really look like?" He pursed his lips and nodded. "Yes."

"Great." I ambled around the tree and found Drinn holding the halfling against a trunk. He still refused to speak to her, and as soon as I was in view, he turned to stare at me, as hungrily as ever. Did he really mean to take a bite out of me? I couldn't imagine what had made him so crazed, unless being in that place had done something to his mind, too. But Drinn and Otsoa didn't seem to be affected.

"What do you want from her? Hm? Why her?" Drinn grabbed the halfling's face and forced him to look at her. "What is she?"

"Born on a green beneath a fairy hill. Was the moon full that night or was the sun shining still?" The halfling wheezed out.

"At least his rhymes are improving," I muttered.

Drinn looked over her shoulder at me, and my anxiety solidified into a cold, hard feeling in my stomach. She knew. She knew what I was, and that I had lied to her for years. She turned away.

"All right, so she's a Changeling. What's that have to do with you?"

"So sweet, so sweet. Like honey from the tree. Just a little taste? Please?"

"A taste of what?" Drinn shook him again. Still there was no answer. She stood up and turned to face us, but when she looked up it was only at Ostoa. I might as well have been invisible. An old wound, a scar left by another person who had been very close to me, split open. The look on Drinn's face was the same. Once they had discovered what I was, I was nothing to them. Worse than nothing. I disgusted them. The Wild stood for everything they hated, the complete abandon, the barbaric and brutal control of anything weaker. And it was part of me. Otsoa discovering me had been different, I hadn't been lying to him for years. Josie, bless her, had forgiven me. Drinn was not so sweet.

"I think I know what he wants," I said. There were few things that would have this kind of pull on a person's mind. I don't know if his exposure to that place had done this to him, or if someone Wild had gotten a hold of him for too long. But now that Drinn knew, I could test my theory. "Stay back with Otsoa."

Drinn made a point of moving away from me as we crossed, her to stand by Otsoa, me to stand by the halfling. I played a quick tune on the flute, creating a bubble of silence around Otsoa and Drinn. No sense in getting everyone riled up. Then I turned to the small man, who was looking up at me with an expression of such hope it nearly broke my heart.

"Here's the deal," I said. "I will give you a taste of the Wild. Just a little. But then you have to answer any question I ask of you, completely honestly. No silly rhymes." I kept my voice friendly, warm. I sat down in front of him, cross-legged. "Now, you know that when we Wild make a deal that it's binding, right? Don't lie to me."

"No, no, no lies. I will answer, no rhymes. I promise." He sounded sincere, and we had nothing else to go on. In a moment he would be as talkative as a jay. I just hoped it would make sense. I began a song on my flute, not a spell song like those I'd learned as an apprentice bard. This song was old, and flowing, and as I played, I tried to pull into it the sunlight and life around me, what little there was of it. Since there was no Wild around me, the song stayed flat and tuneless. Instead, I had to reach inside, to the burning sunlight that was always there. I didn't like tapping into it, it tended to overrun me and anyone near me when I did, so I cautiously allowed the tiniest bit of light into my song.

The flute burst into a cascade of notes that sounded like a rippling stream surrounded by lush trees and bird song. The halfling arched his back and laughed the way only halflings can, a childish laugh that made his cheeks rosy. His eyes glazed over, and he hummed along with the tune. I stopped playing and set down my flute.

"Don't stop, please, just a little more?" He wasn't speaking as crazily as he was before. His voice was slow and lazy.

"Answers first. What is that place?"

"The Wild that Was," he said sleepily, a soft smile on his face.

"The what?"

"The Wild that Was. All that was Wild here is no more. It made that place. It's where the goblins dwell." He wrinkled his nose at me. "They let me stay and serve them, and now and then I get a taste from them, too."

He wasn't speaking in riddles anymore, but it was still making no sense. The goblins had been exiled by the Wild long before elves and humans had fought the Wild here. Even so, the Wild had won that battle. Had the goblins done something to them, and created this place?

"They can give you a taste? Like I can?"

"No, not so good as you. But it's the best we have." He eyed my flute. "Could I have a little more? I told you so much."

"I will give you another taste in a bit. But first, tell me, why does that place hate me?"

"It hates everyone who's born of the Wild. But that's what the masks are for, see? The Masters wear them to keep from going mad. And we wear them to travel in and out."

I tried not to rub my forehead, but it still sounded like so much nonsense to me. "Could you get us some masks?"

His mouth twisted in thought, but his eyes were beginning to clear, so I played a little more of my song. I couldn't keep at this for too long.

"I can get you masks, no problem."

Now for the big question. "Can you show us how to get into the city?"

He clamped his mouth shut and shook his head. It took several minutes of song to loosen his tongue again. I could feel the heat growing stronger in me, but I had to get him back to the lazy, talkative mood. Tufts of green grass sprung up around him, and a small vine climbed the tree behind him, before he resumed the lazy, happy mood. Even then he was evasive.

"I can show you, but it's tricky. I can't promise much."

I nodded, tucked my flute away, and released the silence around Drinn and Otsoa.

"That's not how I remember that going," Otsoa said, eying the halfling who looked ready to drift off to sleep. Otsoa had been subject to one of my outbursts, an all-out Wild song that had driven him and a whole inn, Josie's inn, into a wild party.

"I didn't give him much." I shrugged. "I don't think any of what he said made any sense, but he's agreed to help us."

Drinn's face twisted in pity and disgust as she looked over the hazy halfling. "You mean once this has worn off."

"Look, he asked me to, all right? And he'll be fine," I said. The effects were already fading, and he sat up.

"Better than fine. Better than anything. They just don't understand. Not like we do." He leaned toward me, and I flinched away. "Don't worry, I'll get you some masks, and then show you the door. Then maybe I can taste a little more? I just need my mask back."

"Not going to happen," Drinn said. "So fill us in, so we can decide what we're going to do."

#

"Clearly I'm the one that should go in with him." Drinn was leaning against a tree. This time it was the halfling I held inside a bubble of silence while the rest of us talked. He still looked a little glazed but was starting to fidget with his buttons or the things on his belt. "I'm the most familiar with that place, and I'm not going to knock him unconscious to get what I want."

"You're also the least likely to come back," Otsoa said.

"I can't go in there." I tried to meet Otsoa's eyes, but I didn't want him to see how afraid I was. Then I tried to look at Drinn, but she turned her eyes away, looking down at her nails instead. "I don't even know if the masks will work the way he claims. I might still lose it in there."

"Right. I'll go." Otsoa said it so simply, like it was just walking down the street for a coffee instead of disappearing into a dark dimension filled with goblins.

"I'm sorry." I stepped closer to him. Drinn sighed and turned away. "If I could think of any other way."

"It's fine." He looked confused. "I know it makes you feel crazy, but it didn't do that to me. At least not in the short time I was there. We'll pop over, grab some masks, and pop back."

I nodded and patted his arm. I hoped it would be that simple. Otsoa headed over to the halfling, and I released the silence around him. He looked past Otsoa at me, frowning.

"Are you not coming?" The halfling asked.

"Not until I get a mask," I said. "So make it quick, all right? Come right back and then I can join you over there."

The halfling nodded, his face changing to a simpering smile. "Yes, yes, we'll be right back. The others will be so jealous!" He grabbed hold of Otsoa's sleeve and started reaching for the mask that Otsoa had attached to his belt.

Otsoa snatched it away and held it high over his head. "I'll take care of that part, thanks." He put the mask on, taking time to adjust the straps for his larger head, and then took hold of the halfling's arm. "Right. Back in a flash." And they both disappeared.

I fought to keep from pacing and forced myself to look up at Drinn. She was still looking away, so I could see her graceful, pointed ear, decorated with a set of gold earrings with deep blue stones. Whatever she had been doing before I had run into her again, she must have been succeeding. She still wore her hair back in tight, fancy braids. I could see the first bits of gray hair at her temples, which was unusual for an elf at her age.

"So are we going to talk about this?" I asked her.

"Why, so you can lie to me some more?"

I winced and took a step back. She still wouldn't look at me. "I didn't lie to you," I said, but my words were weak and slow.

"Technically," she said. She raised her hand so it was resting on the wrinkled bark of a tree. "You were hiding the truth, though. I thought you had a scar or were running from a crime or something. But this . . ." She sighed. "I can't believe I was such an idiot."

"You weren't an idiot," I said. "I just let you assume. It was easier."

"How many of your own kind have you killed?" She turned to me then, her eyes dark and intense, boring into me. "I mean, I know you didn't kill any while you were with me. But you're a Warden now. Or is it the other way? Are you letting Wardens die now to protect your kind?"

"No, it's not like that." I backed up another step, wobbling on the stupid tree roots. "I try to help both. If a Warden's getting in over their head, I can help them, give inside information. If some tiny Wild thing that couldn't hurt a fly is in danger, I can help them out too."

"Right, because that's how the Wild works." She rolled her eyes and waved her other hand. She was still holding her dagger. "You know as well as I even the smallest Wild thing is dangerous."

"So are the smallest Free People," I managed to say. My voice was shaking now. A trembling ache was welling up in me, making even my Summer-given flame die down. My muscles tensed, and I looked around to be sure I could run if I needed to.

"I've never seen anyone do that," she said, pointing with the point of her dagger to where the halfling had been lying. "Never. Not even mushrooms gets you that level of desperate. He would have gnawed off his own hand for a taste of you." She turned the dagger point to me, straight at my heart, only an inch away from my leather vest. "If I ever find out that you used that on me."

"Never," I said. "I have never used it on you."

"Would I even remember? I mean, you don't remember when they use it on you."

"He remembered it enough to want to bite me," I said, backing away from her and stumbling on a tree root. I wanted to get out from under the point of her dagger.

"Does Otsoa remember? Does he beg you for it too? I wonder if Josie knows about that."

"He doesn't remember," I mumbled. "And he doesn't want any more."

"And what about you?" Her words just kept plowing into me, like she wasn't even listening to my answers. "Do you still want it?"

I lowered my eyes and slumped. "All the time."

"Oh, and you can't just sing to yourself?"

"That's not how it works." I was hardly speaking, mumbling under my breath.

"You've actually tried, too, haven't you?" She started laughing, a crisp, sharp laugh that made me cringe. "That's so pathetic."

I wanted to tell her to shut up, to stop laughing, that she had no idea how hard it was, but I couldn't talk anymore. I just froze, clenched up from head to toe, waiting for her to go away, like I would if a predator was nearby, and I didn't want it to scent me. Her laughter faded out, but she kept staring at me.

"You are really good at hiding it though. I would never have guessed." She let out another short laugh, then turned and left me there. I listened to the sea breeze whistle through the empty trees and tried to relax my muscles. If the worst of it was that I was no longer an impressive bard and con artist for her, I could live with that, really. I could live with it.

"This is going to be trickier than I thought." Otsoa reappeared in a different spot, still holding the halfling who was trying to wriggle out of his grasp. In his other hand he held three masks, all different shades of brownish-green.

"No tricks, no tricks!" The halfling shouted. "He's just a scaredy cat. Just a few goblins and he runs away." The halfling grunted, trying to get out of Otsoa's grip.

"There's five of them. And they had extra masks on them." Otsoa tossed one to me, and I barely came out of my stiffness in time to catch it and fumbled a few times before snagging the strings.

"That's not suspicious or anything," Drinn said, holding a hand out for a mask. Otsoa didn't give her one.

"I watched this one the whole time, and I made sure the others aren't going to run off and tell, but I suggest we get back quickly. The spell will only hold for so long."

"Right." I pulled the mask on, and Otsoa finally handed one to Drinn, and we jumped over together.

Chapter Eleven

I held my breath, my eyes squinting against the weird pallor of the sky, and waited for the rage to rise within me. Nothing happened. I was afraid, stepping into this unknown world and trusting some random, obviously disturbed stranger to lead us through a goblin-built labyrinth. But I didn't feel like tearing his head off, at least, not at the moment. Five other masked people stood around us, two were halflings, two were elves, and one a dwarf. They stood among the shadow forms of the trees, and the dwarf was actually standing within the tree. The solid wall of the Goblin City stretched out behind them. They also wore patched clothes, lumpy and worn. As one, they all turned their eyes on me.

"All of you sit," I said. The mask was itchy and smelled like sweaty leather. I peered through the eye holes at the hungry crew. "Sit." All of them sat down in a semicircle around us and looked up at me patiently. I turned to Drinn and Otsoa and waved for them to get back. It was Otsoa who put up the bubble of silence around Drinn and himself this time, and I readied my flute again. I was about to test how well it was made. Or how good I was at playing it.

I had worked hard to learn bardic magic. My father had pulled some strings to get me apprenticed to one of the best teachers around, and I wanted to prove I deserved the spot. I hadn't been able to relax my vocal cords enough to pull off the kinds of tricks Josie managed to do, so I'd had to learn to make do with instruments. I'd applied myself doubly hard to those and had managed to match my teacher's skill on the flute. The one thing I hadn't tried often was blending my bardic skills with Wild magic. It was like dumping dry straw on an open fire. I had only done it once, accidentally, and had avoided it ever since.

A little taste would make them happy and compliant, but to feed this many of them, I worried I would have to give out more. Usually it made people excited, joyful, passionate, in the most uncontrollable ways imaginable. But if I could blend just a little Wild with a sleeping spell, maybe I could give them what they wanted, and get them out of our hair at the same time. I started the same way I had for the halfling, just adding a tiny bit of Wild in. I had to add more of the burning light before it began to register on all of their faces. I waited until they were all smiling up at me happily, humming along with my tune.

Then weaving around the main melody, I began adding a few running notes, though nothing strong enough to overpower the main song. It was tricky, but I managed to add the right tones in for a sleeping spell, hidden in the ornamentation. If any of these people had been bards they might have noticed, but after enjoying the Wild song they weren't likely to notice anything. One by one, they slipped to the ground and fell into a deep sleep.

I turned back to Otsoa and Drinn, probably a little too self-satisfied, but I thought I had been impressive. Otsoa was smirking, but Drinn just stared blandly at me.

"So how is he going to lead us into the Goblin City while he's asleep?" Drinn asked. She glared down at the first halfling, who was now snoring on top of one of the other of halflings.

"If we can get him separated, we can shake him awake." I eyed the snorers. "Maybe we can roll him off?"

Drinn reached down and yanked on the halfling's sleeve so he rolled down, plopped on to the dark ground, and kept snoring. Drinn grunted, then nudged him with her boot. He rolled over and squinted up at her.

"I was having such a nice dream," he grumbled.

"What's going on here?" Drinn said, grabbing his shirt front and picking him up off the ground. "How did they know we were coming?"

"The flower watches. The flower by the tower," the halfling squeaked. "We saw you when you arrived. And we haven't had a taste in so long."

"Well no more surprise gangs of friends. Or next time we do more than just put them to sleep." She dropped him on the last word, and he scrambled away from her to hide behind my legs.

"Don't hide behind me, I'm just going to let her," I said to him with a smile.

He frowned and slid away from me as well. He pulled himself to his feet, dusted himself off, and sneered up at us. "No need to be so rude. I have helped you so much, and all you've done is be mean." He stuck his chin out and pouted at Drinn. "I answered all your questions."

"And now you're going to show us the way in," Drinn said, pointing her dagger at the city wall.

"Yes, yes, the way in. Tricky, but I can show you. I can't take you through, no, no, not my place to go inside the walls. I'm just a little goblin." He looked down at the others who still snored away. "None of us are allowed in there for long."

"Only the real goblins stay inside the city?" I asked. Otsoa raised an eyebrow at me.

"Yes," the halfling scowled, and drew the word out into a spiteful hiss. "The goblins and their favorites."

"How do they expect you to behave, when you're inside? Do you have any secret words to say? Do you have to bow to them?" I crouched down again to look the halfling in the face. He had big, round, blue eyes still glazed from sleep and the Wild song, and they looked so innocent.

"Don't look in their eyes, don't raise your head. Only there to get orders and run along." For just a second, his expression cleared, and he looked at me with soft sorrow. "Don't let them see what you are, sweet one. They won't treat you so nice."

I stood up and backed away, then looked down at my arms. I still looked disguised, but then, I hadn't noticed the change when I'd been here before. I looked to Otsoa in a panic.

"Don't worry, you still look like Glade," he said. "Though maybe we should rumple our clothes up some to fit in better."

The halfling giggled. "Yes, yes, they like to be the only ones that look nice. So you have to get a bit messy. Down in the dirt!" He dropped to the ground and started flopping around, laughing as he stirred up the dust.

"I'm not rolling in the grass like a dog," Drinn said. She did mess her clothing up, adjusting the straps so her undertunic stuck out in puffs. Otsoa did get down into the dirt, though he didn't laugh. I whispered a few quick rhymes, casting a few patches of illusion over my clothing to try to match the patched-together look of the 'goblins.'

"Not just a false face," the halfling said.

"What's your name?" I asked him.

"Grinf," he said with a smile. "Do you like it? I picked it myself."

"Fine, we're ready, let's get this over with." Drinn tucked away her knives, but she still glared down at Grinf. "Lead on."

\#

97

We traveled along the wall for what I assumed was the rest of the evening. It was difficult to tell in that place. I don't think the sun ever moved there, just stood still over the horizon in the colorless sky. Gray light filtered through the faint trees, shadows of the naked trees on our side, that we could walk through as though they weren't there. The only thing that was solid other than the sharp grass on the ground was that wall, stretching into the distance. I expected to run into another set of 'goblins,' or even real ones, or to feel that strange anger boiling up inside again. But everything was still and lifeless. We couldn't hear the sea anymore.

"How much farther is it?" Drinn had taken a knife out again and was scraping it along the wall as we walked. The dry scratching was driving me crazy, but it was better than having her drive it into someone else.

"Well you want the door with no traffic, and none of those are any good." He waved his hand at the blank wall as though pointing to doors. "Put you right in the market square or on to Main Street and then everyone will see the new little goblins trying to sneak in without doing any work."

Drinn stopped scraping with her knife, pressed herself against the wall, listening, and felt the seams of the bricks with her fingers. I had seen her find dwarven moon doors in broad daylight with nothing but her fingertips before, so if there was a hidden door there, she should have been able to detect it. She turned around, leaned against the wall, and smiled down at Grinf like he was a child playing make believe.

"There had better be a real door soon," she said, her smile sharp and chilling.

"Yes, yes, just over here." Grinf hurried forward, leading us over the next hill, then stopped and faced another blank section of wall. "Here it is. This will put you in behind the garbage dump. Only little goblins. The others don't like to go there. Then you just follow the yellow bricks. Easy peasy."

"So, where's this door?" I asked.

Drinn half-heartedly ran her hand over the wall, but she didn't look hopeful. Otsoa peered at the wall but didn't take out his wand. He started looking higher, as though calculating what it would take to jump over it.

Grinf huffed, stepped up to the wall, and knocked on it. A thin crack appeared, starting from where he had knocked, up and down along the edges of bricks, until it reached the ground and the top of the wall. Then a section of wall swept out toward us like it was on hinges. We stumbled out of its way as best we could, then stared inside the city. Grinf had told the truth about where we were entering. Mounds of broken furniture, leftover food, torn clothes and all kinds of garbage spread in mounds through the warrens of broken-down walls. Further ahead, the towers of the twisted castle loomed against the dark sky.

"See? Door." Grinf sidled over to me and gazed up with those big blue eyes. "So I can have one last taste?"

I quickly turned my grimace into a smile and nodded, then raised my hand to put a protective silence around the others. Drinn pushed my hand down and moved to stand beside Grinf.

"Not this time. I want to see what all the fuss is about."

"Drinn, I really don't think that's a good idea." I tried to make the spell again, and again she knocked my hand away.

"You weren't too embarrassed to feed a bunch of total strangers," she said. "Let's have it."

"Don't be an idiot," Otsoa said, moving to take her arm and pull her away from me. "You have no idea what you're talking about."

"No, I don't, because she never told me." She snatched her arm away from him and shooed him away. "Go hide in your bubble if you want to. I want to feel this."

"As you like," Otsoa said, raising his hands. He moved away from us and wrapped himself in silence. I stared at Drinn a while longer, but she held her ground, waiting to be impressed.

"Whatever," I said, then raised my flute and started. I was hoping to shock her, at least a little, but she just closed her eyes as the song washed over them. Grinf shuddered happily, and settled on the ground, humming. Drinn swayed to the song and let out a long sigh like she was releasing a load of tension. When I stopped playing, she waited a long time before opening her eyes.

"You like the control too, don't you?" she asked.

"What?" I kept my eyes from hers as I put away my flute.

"You like feeding on the song, being controlled by it like you are in the Wild. But you also like being the one in control." I could hear the smirk in her voice as I turned away. "Which one do you like better?"

I ignored her, patted Grinf on the head, and strode in through the open wall. Otsoa came up beside me, close enough for his arm to brush mine, but since I couldn't read his face through our masks, I couldn't tell what he was thinking. He may have wanted to show me support, or he may have been keeping a closer eye on me. Drinn chuckled to herself and followed. Once she was inside, the wall swung shut again.

The smell was dreadful, rotten food and mildewed furniture, and mixing that with the wet smell of my mask, it made me gag. We picked our way around a few piles and found a few other masked figures with large barrels strapped to their backs. They came up beside the piles, lowered the barrels and dumped more garbage into the mess, then put them on their backs again and headed up a set of stairs into a narrow stone street lined with thin, leaning houses.

"Guess we'll add to the disguise," Otsoa said, pointing to some empty barrels nearby. They were rotten in places, but still looked like they could hold some trash. We strapped them onto our backs and trudged up to the road and out of the dump. The first few blocks of houses were deserted and run-down. A winding path lined with walls rose just high enough to block our view. Not a proper maze, but it may as well have been. The walls were made of the same stone as the outer walls and were covered in strange vines and dark moss. When we reached more solid houses, we passed other masked figures, but no one raised their eyes to look at anything, let alone us, so no one bothered us.

Drinn moved ahead of us, counting bends and turns, then stopping now and then to check the map. The route took us through other clumps of houses. While less thin and rickety than others we had seen, these were surrounded by rotten, moldy gardens. Eventually the narrow street opened up in to a broad avenue of polished stones sprinkled with sparkling golden dust. The walls were cleaner, made from whiter stones, and topped with flowering vines that smelled like honey. The coloring was still dim and faded, but it was clear that these were the only houses being lived in, or at least, the only ones that were being cared for.

"You there! You will not get away with that so easily!" A shrill voice called to us from a large house of glowing blue stone and colored glass. A woman was leaning out of a higher window, wearing a mask like ours, though she was more cleanly dressed than any of the others we had seen.

We froze at a gap in the wall that ran around the house, exchanging glances with each other. Drinn was already pointing in the best direction to run.

"Collect the garbage, fools. Unless you want to get sent back down to latrine duty." She pointed a scrawny feather duster at the bins lined up along the inside of the wall. She kept watch as we took turns filling each other's barrels. Something leaked through mine and down my back. I had to fight to keep from gagging. Once we had collected our burdens, the woman disappeared into the house, and we continued on.

"Maybe we should pick up at a few more places along the way," Otsoa said. "Just to avoid attention?"

"I don't think it's going to help." Drinn motioned over her shoulder with her chin, and I looked back. There were dozens of masked people behind us, of all shapes and sizes. They were doing their best to look like they were supposed to be there, picking up garbage, trimming vines, or sweeping the streets, but I could tell they were watching us. Following us.

"Well, they aren't sounding any alarm," I said hopefully.

"I don't think they care about turning us in," Otsoa said. "I don't think they care about us. Just you."

I felt the blood rush to the pit of my stomach, and I started looking around frantically for a place to hide, but we had just reached an intersection. There were no crevices or corners to hide in, and the streets were quickly filling with masked people waiting there, staring at me with those domed, shiny black eyes.

"That corner," Drinn hissed, pointing. "Now."

I bolted in that direction, not even looking to see what was there or if the others were behind me. The corner led me to a small alley, then to another wide street and three more 'goblins.' I slipped one strap from my shoulder and turned sharply before dropping the other, so my barrel of trash swung out into their faces, bowling them all down the street and giving me time to rush past. I heard feet pounding behind me, then Drinn's throaty shout, giving me directions. We stumbled out into a plaza with a lumpy fountain spurting water into a lopsided bowl.

"This is ridiculous," Otsoa hissed. "We can't just run around forever."

"We don't have to," Drinn snapped. "Just two more blocks." She took us west this time, down one street, across another alley, then back up the next street, keeping close to the wall. She stopped us at the corner, peered around the wall, and motioned toward a grate in the middle of the street. "Down," she barked.

"Oh, please no," I whined.

"Down," she repeated. I grabbed the grate and dragged it out of the way. "Hurry, they're coming."

I took a deep breath, pinched my nose, and jumped down into the sewer.
#

"I hate you," I said as Drinn splashed down beside me. We were standing knee deep in filth in a dark tunnel that was only just high enough to stand in. I had to move aside as Otsoa jumped down beside us, splashing more of the stuff onto me. He gagged, then glared at Drinn.

"Great plan," he said.

"Love you all, too." Drinn shoved past me and started down the tunnel. "Come on before they figure out where we went."

I lost track of the twists and turns we went through in those tunnels, but Drinn pressed ahead without hesitation. The sewers were even more of a maze than the streets above, and I had no idea which direction we were going. After fifteen minutes, I was ready to go back up and face the hordes of hungry goblins.

"How much longer do we have to stay down here? I'm sure we've lost them by now." I tried to grab hold of Drinn's shoulder, but she shrugged me off.

"We're better off down here. I think this place covers your smell." We reached an intersection and she turned left.

"I think she has a point," Otsoa said. He had tied something over his mouth and his voice was even more muffled than it was by the goblin mask. "Don't worry, I can clean us up when we get out."

"If we ever make it out." I followed silently for a few more turns, and then the tunnels opened up into a cistern of some kind, a large open cavern half filled with murky water. Several large pipes led in from all directions, some dumping water in, some drawing it out and piping it who knows where. I knew that the 'goblins' were mad, but they were still people. I couldn't imagine they had stooped to drinking this sludge. Maybe they were using it to water the plants, which would explain how terrible the crops had looked.

"These ones," Drinn said, tapping a large group of pipes leading up and into a narrow tunnel that looked like it ran just underneath the street. "We crawl though here."

"Uh, and just how long do we have to crawl through there?"

Drinn had already shimmied up the pipes and was peering into the hole. "About twenty feet. Then we can go back topside." She looked down at Otsoa. "Got any more glowstones?"

Otsoa fished a few from his bags and tossed one up to her, then handed one to me. "Come on, last stretch."

I looked up at the hole, down at myself and the filth clinging to my clothes and shook my head. "Whatever they sent her to get, it can't be worth all of this. Plus, she's in now. She doesn't really need us to help with this part."

"You don't know that," he said. "Besides, whatever she's in this for, you're in this to help Glenn. Remember that."

"I hate you, too," I said, and he smiled. I had to smile back. "What are you doing this for?"

"I have to make enough to get the approval of Josie's family," he said, tossing a glowstone up and catching it. "This will just about do it."

"Wow. That's so . . ."

"Romantic? Adorable?"

"Pathetic," I said with a laugh. "She doesn't need you to do all that, you know. She'd love you if all you had was the glint in your eyes."

"Yah, but I know how important her family is. Her traditions. You can't tell me she doesn't like that I'm learning all the things." He grinned. "Better get going. We're going to lose her."

I sighed and climbed up into the narrow tunnel. I could get through on my hands and knees, but it wasn't easy. And I wished we hadn't brought the glowing stones along as I saw how many spiders and other creepy things were living in there. Drinn was still scraping through the tunnel in front of me. Ostoa pulled himself in behind.

"Flames, this is going to be tight," he said.

The tunnel was wide enough to let me pass without touching the sides, but only just. I guessed he was scratching his arms or catching his pack along the slimy sides of the tunnel. Compared to the smell of the filth behind us, it wasn't as bad here, mostly musty and moldy. I tried to crawl along as quickly as I could, especially once I noticed light up ahead as Drinn cleared the tunnel. I sped up, but felt a twinge of nausea, and heard Otsoa cursing more behind me with a hissing growl.

"You're trying to shift in here?" I had no idea if he could hear me, as I was facing away from him and tried not to speak too loudly. It was bad enough Drinn had learned about me, I was hoping we could keep his secret.

"I'm stuck." He grunted, and something tore against the side of the wall. "Just let me go long enough to get unstuck."

"Fine. Fine. But you have to change back before the end of the tunnel, all right? Or maybe the goblins will think you're a good dessert once they're done with me."

"Lucky I can run way faster than you when I'm a cat then," he chuckled.

The nausea grew and I stopped fighting it. I didn't hear him change, but as we continued forward, the scraping sounds stopped. In fact, there was no sound from him at all now. I reached the end of the tunnel which opened into another large cistern, this one much cleaner. Drinn was standing on a catwalk that ran around the cisterna, watching the opening. She nodded at a ladder that led to a large grate on the ceiling.

"It's just up there," she said. "You guys could wait here for me."

I felt Otsoa come up behind me. He growled softly, and I pulled hard against the weird swirling in my stomach. Choosing my steps carefully, I climbed out of the tunnel, then looked back to make sure it was Otsoa looking out at me and not a jaguar. He had to squeeze through, bumping his shoulders on the edges, but he pushed out and stood beside us on the metal walkway.

"So, how exactly did you find this place?" Otsoa folded his arms and tilted his head. "You weren't following a map during the chase."

Drinn didn't answer. Instead, she mirrored Otsoa's pose and waited.

"Have you been here before?" I couldn't imagine any other reason she would know the sewer system. She hadn't known how to get into the city. But she had known about the masks, or at least, the thing she had that had been part of a mask.

"No, I have never been here before. And I can't tell you how I knew the sewers. You wouldn't believe anything I said anyway." Drinn unfolded her arms and started getting ready to climb out. She drew on a pair of dark gloves then removed all the things hanging from her belt and set them in a niche in the wall. "You don't have to worry about it anyway. We're here. I will climb up, find the weapon, and climb back down. Then we can all make a quick getaway." She tapped the mask on her face.

"And what guarantees you don't climb up, grab the weapon, and disappear without us?" Otsoa said.

Drinn rolled her eyes. "Because even if I blinked back to the real world, I'd still be stuck in the middle of nowhere by the North Tower. I don't know how to open that thing we used to get here. You'd catch up to me in no time. Stop being so paranoid."

"We still don't know what's up there," I said, stepping between them. "You might still need our help to get whatever the weapon is. Or even to figure out what it is."

"If you insist, but for Flame's sake, can you at least go invisible? We need this part to go smoothly."

"All right, so we go in invisible, we find the weapon, and we blink back to our world. No problem." Otsoa was checking the tears on his sleeves. A few specks of blood, but they were only scrapes, which he cleaned up quickly.

"You guys should leave as much down here as you can. Less noise, less chance of getting snagged on something."

Otsoa held his bag close and frowned at her. "And then what happens if I need to cast something?"

"Bring your wand." She shrugged. "And whatever potions you can keep in your pockets, but only what you really need."

He sighed, but obliged, setting down the bag and digging out a few small vials, then removed his belt entirely, leaving it next to Drinn's things on the wall. I didn't have much on my belt, and my flute tucked away neatly in my pocket.

Once they were ready, I raised my flute and prepared to play us out of sight. "Just remember, no sudden movements, and try not to bump into anything. And no spellcasting. It will interfere with my spell." They both nodded, and I played a quiet melody that slowly faded into silence. All three of us faded into mere shadows, then we started up the ladder together.

#

It was a longer climb up than I expected. The grate at the top was a round, heavy metal circle with small drain holes in it. Drinn slid the grate aside with expert grace and in complete silence. We scrambled up onto a spotless shining marble floor in a hall so tall I couldn't see the ceiling. Wide columns spread out around us carved to look like tree trunks. Between the columns sat pedestals covered in glass cases, hundreds of them, each with something different spotlighted by a glow that emanated from the tops of the columns. We had come up beside a display of what looked like large, serrated teeth.

The lighting cast long shadows around us and kept us from being completely invisible. I could see the vague outlines of Drinn and Otsoa examining the objects around us. Otsoa pointed to the plaque under the array of teeth.

"Dragon Teeth," it read. "Gathered from east of the tower, on the 60th day of Winter, 856 After the Breaking."

Drinn held her hand up, motioned for us to stay put, and stepped away down the row of pedestals. Her steps made no sound. I could hear air moving through the place and could imagine any step I took echoing forever through the columns. I chewed my lip and tapped a rhythm on my leg, anything to keep from shuffling my feet with nervous energy. The situation felt wrong, and not just because this massive showroom was conspicuously empty and unguarded without even a simple spell to detect movement.

After six columns, I lost sight of Drinn in the dimness. Otsoa moved to follow her, but I grabbed his arm. We would want to be close to the grate if something went wrong, and I didn't want to lose sight of them both.

There was a soft click, and the glass top on one of the pedestals raised up and over the thing on display and settled softly on the floor. The item was several yards away, so I couldn't really see it. It looked like a metal sphere, about the size of her head.

I frowned and swallowed hard. It was all too convenient. She had known precisely where to go once we were inside the city, running us through the streets and then underground without a thought. And now she had gone straight to the thing we needed.

A shrill whistle pierced the air, and Drinn dropped the sphere with a clang. She bolted back to us, losing the invisibility as she ran.

"Let's get out of here, now!" She slid to a stop at the grate.

I touched the mask, and tried to push back to our realm. Nothing happened. In a panic I swung my arms around trying to find the others, and slapped Otsoa's cheek.

"Hey," he cried out.

"It's not working," I said, trying to find Drinn.

"No kidding," she said, taking my hand. "Maybe it won't work inside the room?" Drinn cursed, trying to drag the grate up, but it wouldn't budge. "This isn't good."

"I beg to differ, I think things are working exactly as they should," a voice said out of the darkness. "I do have to give you credit, however. So few people make it this far. You will have to tell me all about it."

Light flooded the room, and I covered my eyes. When I lowered my hands, we were all visible again, and another person was standing with us. He was tall, over six feet, dwarfing the three of us. His hair was long, and white, and hovered around his head in cascading waves. He wore a perfectly white suit with wide lapels made of shining silk and a pristine, frilly shirt that fit him like an expertly crafted glove, topped off with a long white cape. Over the top half of his face rested a gold filigree mask, but instead of the domed eyes on our own masks, his eyes, his real eyes, were solid black orbs.

"That is a goblin," I said to Drinn, without taking my eyes from him.

"You can put that back now," he said to Drinn. He held out a long, thin hand adorned with two large gold rings encrusted with jewels, and pointed at the sphere. She walked back to where she had dropped it and lifted it back into his place. The glass dome floated up and back over the item. He looked over us like he was studying one of his treasures, trying to gauge how much we were worth. His eyes paused on me, and a small smile twisted his lips, before he turned away from us and started walking down the row. When he moved, an invisible grip wrapped around us so tight that I couldn't raise my arms. It forced us to follow, dragging us along the floor like he was pulling us on a sled.

"I have so many questions," he said. His voice was cold and clear, like a mountain stream, and there was something deliciously crisp about it that made me want to drink in more. "How did you learn about the masks? Where did you get them? Who showed you the way into the city? But really, I think I will have to start with the most important thing. Everything else can wait." He dragged us through large double doors into another room, this one with a purple carpet down the center leading to an elaborate throne. There were no people here either, but it was lit much more brightly, with tall red and purple glass windows stretching from floor to ceiling every few feet.

He turned when he reached the throne and sat down, sprawling back on the chair and tossing one leg over the armrest. He released his grip on us and dropped us onto the carpet. My legs went weak, and I slumped on to the ground beside my companions, feeling like a puppet whose strings were cut, or a limp rag doll.

"Play for me," he commanded, and hoisted me to my feet again with a flick of his finger. I waited to see if he would make me raise my flute to my lips, but he waited, staring at me with those solid black eyes.

I nodded, pulled out my flute, and began to play, something similar to what I had played for the pretend goblins, but he clicked his tongue and shook his head.

"Ah, that may work for the boorish minions out there," he said with a lazy wave of his hand. "But not for me. You know what I want to hear."

I stopped and looked down at Otsoa. "Let them stop their ears," I said, motioning to Otsoa with my chin. "They don't want to hear it."

Drinn started to argue, but at a motion from the goblin she choked on the words. He looked her over, then examined Otsoa again. A familiar tug of nausea pulled at me, and I glared down at him and shook my head. This was not the time.

"Their loss," the goblin said. "And you may call me Dominus."

I refrained from rolling my eyes. "Otsoa, Drinn, cover your ears." The goblin released them long enough to allow the movement, and then clamped down on them enough to make him grunt in pain. I'm sure the goblin had fed on Wild song before, though I suppose it had been a long time. Wild song could be played many different ways, full of sleepy summer days or blazing fierce anger, and they could all be dangerous to the listener. I raised my flute to my lips and jumped full bore into the fiercest Wild song I knew.

As soon as the music swept over him, the goblin's eyes lit up a deep green and grew wide. He sat up on his throne and listened intently, his eyes glued to my fingers as they flew over the holes of the flute. His composure only made me angrier, and I poured all of the heat I could from the Wild sun at my heart into that song. Slowly, a warm, wide smile spread across his face, and he reached down beside the throne and brought a small fiddle to his shoulder. He bobbed his head a few times to count the rhythm, and then he joined in on the song, providing a perfect and furious counterpoint to the freewheeling jig I was flying through.

When it reached a crescendo, I felt the flute fly out of my hands. It wheeled up into the air where it was joined by the fiddle, and they swirled around each other. My song slowed, but the goblin shook his head.

"No, just keeping the song flowing. It will play just fine." He stepped down from the throne and with long, languid steps came to stand right in front of me. He reached a thin hand out and stroked my chin. "Such fire. I am so glad you came to me. Now, sweet one, let my song in."

With those words, his song changed, still complementing mine but filled with a sharpness that stabbed straight through me. I expected my senses to catch fire, flooding with sound and feeling until it overloaded me and knocked me unconscious like Wild song could. Instead, every sense focused into a fine point, shutting out Otsoa, Drinn, and the room—even making me forget about Glenn and Roya and what we were doing there. There was only the music, and the goblin.

Our eyes locked. He slid his hand down my shoulder and along my arm. He clasped my hand, and we began to dance. This was not the unfettered dance of the Wild. This was a metered dance with clear steps and complex figures. We swept out onto the floor, tracing patterns shaped like leaves and the branches of trees and turning in tight circles with our arms entwined. My heart picked up to match the rhythm of the song. Each touch from him, each gaze, both stirred up the fire within me and trained it tighter, like sunlight through a lens. I was aware of everything, so long as it was connected to Dominus, every tiny variance in music, the sound of his breath, even the beating of his heart.

When the song finally ended, it may have been minutes or hours, I couldn't tell, he stayed holding me around the waist and staring into my eyes. My illusion had melted away sometime during the dance, and I could see my brilliant green eyes reflected in his glossy ones. They faded back to black.

"Now, sweetness, can you see why we were driven away from the Wild and left to rot in this wasteland?"

I nodded, too breathless to answer.

"I'm sure you have many more questions, but you should rest now," he said, letting me go. "There will be many more dances and many more chances to talk. I suppose you would prefer I keep your friends in good health?"

"Yes, please, your majesty," I answered, worried somewhere in the back of my mind about how sincere it sounded.

"That can be arranged, especially in exchange for such a delicious flame as you." He brushed my cheek again, then took me by the hand and led me to a door in the side of the room. It opened before we reached it. Inside was a lavish space dominated by a massive bed with posts and curtains. I didn't notice anything else. I moved inside, curled up on the bed, and fell asleep.

#

When I woke, I was in different clothes. I wore a long pale green chiffon nightgown, and my hair was loose. A chill spread through me, chasing away the fire from before. Had Dominus changed me in my sleep, or just commanded one of his minions to do it?

Drinn was curled up in a large, overstuffed chair in the corner, and Otsoa was sprawled out on a rug on the floor, snoring loudly. I sat up and stretched, and Otsoa sat bolt upright like he was ready to jump whatever had moved in the room.

"Easy, tiger," I said, patting his head. "It's just me."

"I'm not a tiger," he grumbled, shoving my hand away.

"'Easy, jaguar,' doesn't have the same ring to it."

"Hate to tell you, but he puts people to sleep better than you do." He hopped up and took a seat beside me on the bed. "He took our masks. And the map. And my wand. And he was not very polite about it."

I turned to him sharply. "Are you all right? Is Drinn—"

"She's fine. I'm fine. We're just a little bruised." He frowned at me. "What happened? What was that whole . . . dance thing? He destroyed your illusion."

I took a deep breath, tried to think of the words to describe what I had felt, and took another deep breath. He was staring at my hair. I ran my hands over it, but it fluffed back up right away. I tried to pull my hands into my sleeves, but I could still see the glow through the thin linen.

Otsoa raised an eyebrow. "So, was that Wild magic? Are you all right?"

I shrugged. "I don't know. I've never—it was never like that before."

"And how was he able to control the rest of us?" Otsoa was grumbling, the way he did when he found a spell he couldn't unravel. "I mean, he clearly couldn't do with us what he did with you, but I've never seen a Wild creature just take hold of one of the Free People like that. How is he doing that?"

"I have no idea."

"How do we even start to find our way out if he can just toss us around like dolls?" He hopped off the bed and started pacing.

I didn't want to confess to him that there was going to be no way out for me. I wondered if I could somehow convince Dominus to let them go in exchange for more music, but I knew I wasn't in a position to bargain. Not when I wanted the dance this badly.

"I can try and keep his complete attention, maybe get him to only take me from the room. She could sneak you guys out." I nodded toward Drinn.

"And leave you here?" He shook his head. "Not on your life. I don't like what he's got planned for you." He frowned at me. "I don't like that you love it here."

"That's not fair," I said, jumping off the bed. The room was huge, and the carpet felt like clouds beneath my bare feet. Everything was bright white or lively green, including the massive wardrobe that took up most of the wall across from the bed. I swung the doors open to find several beautiful gowns and matching slippers. "I mean, look how hard he's trying."

"Please don't tell me you've fallen for that creep."

"Of course not," I said slamming the wardrobe closed. Drinn startled awake and almost fell out of the chair. "You all right, Drinn?"

"Yah, fantastic." She righted herself on the chair and took in our surroundings as well. "So do you have a plan yet? Or are you just deciding what to wear when he makes you Queen of the Goblins?"

"There's no white gown in here, so I don't hear wedding bells just yet." I was trying to keep up the levity of the conversation, but my words sounded hollow. Beside the bed and the massive wardrobe, there were two large stuffed chairs with a small table between them. There was a lamp on the table, but it wasn't lit. I wasn't sure where the light in the room was coming from, but it was as bright as day.

"We should work on getting out before he comes back. It didn't sound like he left any guards, just the locked door." Otsoa moved to the door and put his ear against it. "Still sounds clear."

"If we can get back underground, we should be able to find a way out," Drinn said.

"How do you know that?" I tilted my head and focused on Drinn. "How did you know any of this? You knew how to use the masks, you knew exactly how to get in here, exactly where to find . . . Whatever that thing was that you were going to steal." I ticked off the suspicions on my fingers as I stepped toward her. She looked up at me with her perfect poker face, not even blinking.

111

"Right. I was prepared. Unlike you. I thought you were supposed to be the expert on these goblins. Did you know they could puppet us like we're toys? Or that they would be addicted to your song? Might have been nice to know that ahead of time." Her face never changed, but her voice was dripping with stinging venom.

Otsoa jiggled the door handle, then shook it hard, then punched the door.

"What's wrong with you?" I asked him.

"I don't like being locked in," he snapped. When he turned to me his eyes didn't focus on me. Instead, they glanced over me and over the whole room, never settling in one place.

"Take a deep breath. We're going to get out." I set my hand over the pendant on his chest and tried to pull him back into a calm. He pulled away from me with a sour look on his face.

"Don't do that right now. You still smell like him." He stalked over to the corner of the room to the other stuffed chair and sat down with a huff.

This didn't bode well. We might all tear each other apart before the goblin would try to kill us. I waved at the door and looked at Drinn. "You wanna give this a whirl?"

Drinn shrugged, went over to the door, and started probing it. She took a long time, going over some spots more than once, and finally shoved away from the door. "Flames and iron, this is impossible," she growled. "It's not just locked; it's sealed. Maybe wand boy can take another crack at it."

Otsoa let out a bitter chuckle but got up and moved back to the door. "There's not a whole lot I can do without my wand, you know. And I left behind my new bag of materials," he grumbled. Still, he laid his hands against the door and began to chant a spell. A blue glow spread out from his hands over the door, but it dissipated almost immediately. He started chanting louder, using older words and focusing on his pronunciation with a precision I rarely heard him use. Rather than grow in strength, the magic would spread and then fade away like the door was absorbing everything he put into it.

"There's one other thing we could try." I waited for Otsoa to move aside, then stepped up to the door and knocked. The door swung open, but the throne room was not empty as Otsoa had thought. The goblin was there, just a few feet from the door, and several of the pretend goblins were standing around him, frozen in various poses of obeisance to their lord.

"I was wondering how long that would take you." The goblin snapped his fingers and his minions rushed into the room. There were all elves this time, tall and strong, and they grabbed hold of each of us and shoved masks on to our faces before dragging us out into the throne room. "I'm sure you're all famished. Let's have some breakfast, and we can get some questions answered."

He took hold of us with that invisible hand and sat us around a table set with shining silverware and gold-rimmed plates. The candelabras were etched with the names of elvish families that had died out centuries ago, and I was sure that if I could read the Old Human words on the plates, it would show them to be just as old. The goblin made me raise my hand and take one of the pastries, even making me chew it until I made it clear I was willing to do that much on my own. I could see the anger smoldering in Drinn's eyes as he forced her drink from a teacup with her pinky out, and the look of a caged animal in Otsoa's face as he gingerly sliced into some ham. They weren't going to put up with this for long.

This was the stuff of my nightmares. Changelings fell prey to this kind of control all the time, which is why I had determined to stay as far away from the Wild as I could when I was younger. I knew more than a few who had ended up as permanent pets to a powerful Wild being. When I became a Warden, I learned that they really only controlled their pets when they were paying attention, and otherwise they could do as they pleased. If I didn't do anything to attract attention, he would likely leave me alone. I had Dominus's complete attention, unfortunately.

When we finished eating, he clapped his hands and summoned the minions back. "All right, class time." He made us all stand, and the minions pulled away the table and arranged the chairs in a row, while a few others pulled a slate board into place beside the goblin. Another presented him with a long piece of chalk, which the goblin didn't touch, instead making it float into the air and over to the slate. Then he made us sit in our seats, upright and attentive.

"You first," he said, dragging Drinn's chair forward so she was seated in front of us. "Why this?" An image of the sphere Drinn had tried to take appeared on the slate. All the chalk did was draw a circle around it. "It's useless to you. Even to that one who has enough Wild blood to make such

113

delicious songs couldn't get this thing to work. So why risk so much to steal it from me?"

"That's what I was sent to get," Drinn answered. Her voice was forced, and it sounded like she was reading from a script. "I don't know what they want with it."

"Wrong answer," the goblin said cheerily, and flung Drinn and the chair across the room. She slammed into the wall, still attached to the seat and unable to move her arms to shield her head from banging against the stone. Then he slid her chair back to its place in front of us. I cringed to see the side of her face was red and blood trickled down from her temple. "Now, try again."

I tried to think of one of our old cons, a story we could both at least try to fool Dominus with, but my mind was foggy. I missed the clarity of the dance with him, and then my heart sank with the realization of just how hooked I was. Drinn clamped her mouth shut and turned her head away. I wanted to cheer for her determination.

"Oh, I don't recommend you shut down on me already." The goblin crouched down so his face was only inches from Drinn's. "We were only beginning to have fun, and I'd hate to have to end it so soon. But if you do not give me the answers I want, I will kill you and the human and move on."

For an instant, Drinn's eyes jumped around and found mine, and she was afraid, really afraid. Then she closed her eyes and clenched her jaw shut. The goblin must have been pressing his magic into her to make her talk, but she fought against it, the muscles in her neck straining, a low moan escaping her clamped lips. She writhed and moaned again, and I couldn't hold back anymore.

"There are nicer ways to ask," I said. Rather than sound enticing, my voice came out shaky. "Do you want me to give it a try?"

He stared down at Drinn with hard, blank eyes, then turned to look at me with a wide grin. "I would very much love to watch you try. Or you could volunteer the information. It would save me from dealing with these fools."

"They didn't tell us exactly what to take. She's the only one that knew any details," I said, shaking my head frantically. Drinn's eyes narrowed at me.

I swallowed hard. He released me from his control and relaxed his grip on Drinn. She sat up, panting, and turned to watch me step toward her. I tried to reassure her with my eyes and with a small twitch of my mouth that I wasn't going to do anything to her, and that she just needed to play along. I wasn't sure she understood, but the fear in her eyes faded, replaced by the cold anger she had stabbed me with before.

Pulling out my flute, I began the slow, intoxicating song I had played for Grinf and his companions. I didn't try to lace it with a sleeping spell this time, terrified that the goblin would know if I tried to play two tricks at once. Drinn's body relaxed instantly, and a lazy smile spread over her face. I lowered my flute, and brushed the hair away from her wound, whispering a quick rhyme to seal up the gash.

"Drinn, why were you trying to steal that sphere?"

"Glade, thanks, that feels so much better." Drinn's words slurred, and she lolled her head back to look at me. I suppressed a smile. She was playing along perfectly.

"I'm glad. I know he wasn't playing nice. So I need you to tell me why they hired you to steal that thing."

"I promised I wouldn't tell." She pressed her lips together and shook her head.

"It's all right, you can tell us now. I won't tell them you broke your promise."

"Can't. Made a promise to one of your kind. You can't go back on those. They *know*." She whispered the last words and then giggled.

"What?" I backed away a step. If she was going to make up a story, I wished she hadn't chosen to bring the Wild into it. The goblin was behind me. He wrapped his hands over my shoulders and spoke into my ear.

"Who exactly are you working for?" he asked.

"Not the Wild," I answered. "At least, I'm not."

"It doesn't matter. I failed. So they're going to kill me. Or he'll kill me. I'm dead either way." Drinn shrugged. "So whatever."

I gripped my flute so tight it creaked. Maybe she wasn't making it up. I hadn't given her that much Wild magic, no more than she had experienced before, and it hadn't done this to her. The mixture of Wild magic and the goblin's power must have muddled her more than usual.

"Ah, well, it's so much nicer when the victims don't fight their fate." The goblin released me, then turned to Otsoa. "I imagine you will have a few objections. You'll have to lodge your complaints later. Now it's time to get ready for the festivities."

"Festivities?" I half-smiled, but the rest of me shivered at the way he said it.

"Yes, it's not every day I get a showpiece like you in my collection. We'll keep these two around for demonstration purposes." He looked me over, a strange smile on his face. "You're not going to try and run now, are you? You'll be a good girl and take them into the room and get yourselves all dressed and ready for tonight?"

I nodded, smiling wider to hide my cringe as he caressed my cheek again.

"Good girl."

Chapter Twelve

I helped Drinn back to the room. Otsoa followed, growling under his breath when the minions shut the door behind us. The lock clicked into place, and minions shuffled around on the outside, taking guard positions surrounding the door. Drinn stumbled to the floor, then rolled over to look up at us and laughed frantically.

"This isn't funny," I rasped at her. "If that was a lie it was a stupid one to tell here. And if you weren't lying—"

"You should have seen your faces." She rolled back and sat up on the floor. "Well if you two bought it I'm sure he did, too."

It wasn't an answer. And I was going to get a straight answer. "Look at me Drinn. Who hired you to do this?"

"You were there. You know who hired me." She looked away.

I grabbed her shoulders and forced her to look me in the face. "And who hired Negri? Why were they looking for us in Rhiodeja?"

"It doesn't matter. We're not getting what we came for. And Negri hired us the way he did to protect whoever he works for." She shoved my hands off her shoulders. "You have a better way to not have to explain what we were doing here? Dominus can understand how binding a deal with the Wild is."

Still no 'yes or no.' Still no straight answer. I squashed a flare of anger and stood up. "Come on, we don't have a lot of time." I stepped around her and headed to the bed. There were three strange outfits arrayed there: a long, dark robe embroidered with star constellations, a suit of dark armor made of small metal plates, and a long, green gown decorated in a scale pattern. "We have to get cleaned up for his guests."

"So what are these festivities?" Otsoa asked. He was still standing by the door, arms folded across his chest, staring down at the amused Drinn.

"He's showing off his collection. I'm guessing I'm the new centerpiece." I tossed the black armor to Drinn. It left a tingling on my fingers. Iron had that effect on Wild things. It was the armor of a true Iron Knight, the cleric warriors who had fought the Wild in the Fairy Wars. I picked up the green gown and held it up to examine it. It was made of woven silk, probably Wild silk, which would change colors under sunlight or moonlight to blend in with the surroundings. It was light as a feather and made in a style I had never seen before.

"I'm supposed to wear that?" Otsoa came to stand beside me and looked down at the long robe laid out on the bed. I had never seen him wear anything more formal than a non-leather tunic, and that was only for dinner with Josie.

I looked over his sewer-tained clothes. "Well, you are looking a little shabby. Though I guess a change of clothes won't really do anything about the smell."

"Glade, we need to get out of here. That creature is going to kill us."

"No, he's going to kill you. He's going to put me under glass in his museum of Wild artifacts and parade me out when he has visitors." I held the gown up to my body and frowned at how low it was going to be. It was designed to be off the shoulder, and there was no under-dress to wear with it.

"Glade, please, be serious."

"I am being serious." I lowered the dress and looked up at him. His eyes were wide and pleading, his mouth flattened to a thin line. "Look, he'll be distracted during the festivities. We just have to watch for a chance to escape and jump on it."

"I don't like it." He grabbed the weird robes from the bed. "Surprised he didn't include a pointy hat and a wand." He stomped over to the wardrobe and propped the doors open as cover while he changed.

Drinn was still chuckling and halfway into the armor. In one shimmying motion, she slipped the armor down to her hips and slid her tunic to the ground. The armor fit strangely. Constructed for a man, it was too large across her shoulders but pressed flat against her chest and pinched her hips.

"How do I look?" she asked. "Good enough to join you in that amazing dance?"

"Where'd you come up with that story?" I started imitating Drinn's way of getting changed, but my gown was tighter than her armor, so I ended up having to contort and wiggle quite a bit more.

"Huh? Oh come on, it's the perfect excuse. Of course the Wild would want their stuff back, and if they had bound me to secrecy, I wouldn't be able to talk about it." She approached me from behind. "Do you need help getting that on?" Her voice was muffled through the fabric.

"No." I managed to force it down over my shoulders and I turned to look at her. "I got it."

118

"Sure." She was staring at me. "That color goes well with your, uh, new skin look."

I rolled my eyes and turned away from her again as I pulled the gown down, then fought to get my trousers off. The gown fit me perfectly, and when I looked at my arm through the translucent green fabric, my skin did look different. The amber glow filtered through the fabric like sunlight through leaves.

"It's the masks!" Otsoa exclaimed. He stumbled out from behind the wardrobe door, still pulling on the robe, his pants around his ankles. We both turned to stare at him, and he blushed, needlessly since we couldn't see anything through the robe. I was briefly jealous that his outfit was more covering than my own. He turned around to finish tying and buttoning everything and kick off his pants, then turned back to face us with more composure. "The mask the goblin wears. That has to be it. It's the masks."

"What are you talking about?" I asked.

"That's how he's controlling us." Otsoa lowered his voice and glanced at the door. "That's how he controls all of them. He's only doing it when we have the masks on. Then when we're in here he takes them off us so we can't blink back to our world and run while he's not paying attention."

"How in the free realm did you come up with that?" Drinn rattled as she put her hands on her armor-clad hips.

"It wasn't making sense. The Wild can control their own kind, sure, but they don't have that kind of control over the free races, not without songs or whatever, right?" He looked at me for confirmation, and I nodded slowly. "So they had to be using something to keep them controlled when they weren't playing their songs. It has to be the masks."

"They do also protect me from the weird rage thing," I said.

"Do they? Or is it just being inside the city? Anyway, that's not the point right now. If we can get off our masks—"

"Or get the mask off him," Drinn added.

"Right, sure, because that would be easier," Otsoa snapped. "Either way, we have a chance to get away."

"She could do it when they dance again. She was certainly close enough," Drinn said, nodding at me.

"She wasn't exactly herself then," Otsoa said.

119

"I'm right here guys," I said. "But yes, Otsoa's right, I might not have the presence of mind to try something like that."

"Fine, then, we'll all watch for an opportunity." Drinn shrugged. "I still think you're the best bet though. I couldn't move an inch when he had us out there. But he seems to think he can control you just with the sweet, sweet taste of his music."

I looked away from them, not wanting them to see the worry in my eyes. I wanted to think that I could keep my wits through the powerful magic that happened when my song mixed with the goblin's. It was certainly better than Wild song by itself, which overran the mind and blacked out any thoughts or memories. But it was still all-consuming. It was like there was nothing in the world but he and I, like nothing else mattered.

"Everyone just keep their eyes open and their minds sharp, alright? This is probably our last chance." Otsoa took a deep breath, then clapped his hands together. "I think I have a plan for a distraction. I just don't know if it will work."

"What are you thinking?" I asked him.

He scooped up his pants and pulled a page from the pocket. "Remember this thing?"

"You're joking, right?" Drinn rolled her eyes, then spun away to pull on to the black boots by the bed.

"I really think it will work. Though some of the calculations are off, and there is a problem with their logic . . ."

"I have no idea what you're talking about," I said, raising my hands.

"Well, even if it doesn't work as a spell, I can still cause enough of a distraction."

"We should have a signal, so we'll know when to make a break for it," I said.

"Right." He thought a moment. "We couldn't move much more than our eyes. I'll catch your eye and wink at you, if I can. If not, at least I can try and growl."

#

I'd taken part in my fair share of performances, enough so that I was rarely nervous in front of a crowd while I was playing. But the minutes leading up to the show still gnawed at the pit of my stomach like an angry gopher. While we waited for the goblin to return for us, my nerves started to get the better of me, and I paced the room.

Drinn lounged on one of the chairs and snickered at me. "What are you nervous about? It's not like it's going to be you performing. You'll just be a puppet on his strings."

I thought for a moment about trying to explain it to her. It wasn't just him controlling me, it was a combination of our songs that drove the dance and controlled us both, flowing through and around us. But she wouldn't have understood, and Otsoa would just worry more about trusting my part of the plan.

"They're coming," Otsoa said. There was a scurry of feet, and the door swung open. The elvish guards rushed in again, shoved the masks onto our faces, and dragged us out into the throne room.

The goblin waited there and took a long, slow time checking us over. He adjusted Drinn's hair, loosening her braids and pulling the black tresses into a single ponytail. He adjusted Otsoa's robes, tightening the silver belt at his waist. Dominus even managed to tame my hair, getting it to fall down around my shoulders in waves. He had changed as well, his long tunic and wide trousers were the same color green as my gown, and he wore a long cape that was striped like bat wings.

Once he was satisfied, he took a step back and looked at the finished product. "This is going to be a real treat. I've only been able to show off a bunch of rusted old relics to those old fools, and there are few of them they haven't seen before. But this, a real live Wild creature, and one skilled in music? They'll never beat that."

He waved for us to follow him but didn't take control of us. The masked thugs behind him were enough to ensure that we shuffled along after him, back to the museum full of Wild relics. He turned right when we entered along a wall hung with large frames that held small Wild things pinned and mounted like butterflies.

I swallowed hard. "I doubt anyone could rival your collection."

"It is extensive, true, and I do have some spectacular pieces. But most of them are common, ordinary things. I mean who doesn't have a set of flower goblets or a few alettas for lanterns." As he spoke, we passed by the things he mentioned. The goblets were formed from giant tulip blossoms colored the deepest blood red, grown into the shape of thin stemmed glasses and frozen in the height of beauty. The alettas, tiny, winged people shining blue, green, and purple peered out at us through the crystal-clear glass of lanterns, their dragonfly wings trembling.

Otsoa paused, staring up at the small lanterns, a deep frown creasing his face. I tried to get a good look at them too before we moved on, to see if there was an easy way to get them open, but the next case drew my attention. Inside was a small mirror, not made from glass, but a thin slab of ice with sharp snowflake edges. Instead of my golden glowing skin and brilliant green eyes, my reflection had snow-white skin and eyes the palest blue of ice over a clear stream. The face mirrored my surprise, but instead of leaning closer as I did to examine it, my reflection backed away and ran off, leaving me looking at a blank piece of ice.

"It's trickier keeping hold of live ones, of course," the goblin continued. If he had noticed that Otsoa and I were distracted, he didn't show it. "Keeping them fed, giving them the sunlight they need, all those sorts of things."

A flash of anger boiled up in me, but I made sure I controlled the expression on my face before I turned back to him. "And then there's the madness, of course."

He paused and looked back at me, making everyone in the group stop. I thought the guards held their breath. "Are you feeling alright, my dear? The effects are not so strong in the city, and I had hoped we'd been giving you enough mask time to mitigate that." He cupped my chin in his hand and looked into my eyes.

"I'm feeling fine." I smiled my brightest, and he smiled back showing all his brilliant white teeth.

"Good. Let me show you to your stage." A large aisle opened to our left between the rows of two-foot square glass boxes covering the items on the pedestals. The aisle led to a twenty-foot wide circle covered by a massive glass dome. The lighting around us was the same, sterile bright light as our prison room and the throne room. But inside, the dome was flooded with warm sunlight. At the far side stood a miniature version of the North Tower, the way it would have looked before it was destroyed. Miniature pine trees were planted around the right side of the dome and the floor was covered with pine needs and dirt. On the other side was the sea, rolling up onto the ground in small waves.

Dominus opened a panel in the side of the dome, which had looked completely seamless before, and waved us inside. "Go on, get comfortable in the space. We are going to do a reenactment, and you'll need to be familiar with the setting." We filed into the dome, and I breathed a sigh of relief that we didn't shrink down to match the size of the set. It smelled like pine and salt water.

"How long do we have to prepare?" I took a turn around the space. My shaky voice echoed back to me.

"They should all be here within the hour. Feel free to dress up the set while you wait." He shut the door on us, and it disappeared, somehow sealing us inside completely.

Otsoa growled under his breath and started pacing. Drinn inched closer to me, her arms wrapped tightly around herself like she was trying to keep warm.

I couldn't tell where the light was coming from, but it felt like real sunlight. I wondered if the cell extended all the way to the roof and out, but even then, it should only be bringing in the weird twilight of this creepy land and not honest, bright sunlight. I stretched my hands out around me and soaked up the warmth. Otsoa started pacing.

I watched him, not liking the distracted look in his eyes, and pulled at him through our bond. He slowed down, eventually moving to lean against the glass. It was helping, but I had to keep hold of it. Every time I tried to loosen up, he would tense up again. He turned around and glared at me.

"Don't get any ideas, all right? It's bad enough he's puppeting us, I'm not going to put up with it from you too."

"I was just trying to help," I mumbled. "Do you think you could make your distraction work from in here? Or are we going to wait until we're on the way back to the room?"

He squinted up into the light and nodded. "We should be able to get it to go off in here. Though I don't like the idea of facing more than one of those creatures."

"We just need Dominus to let us go long enough to blink away. Even if they follow us back to our world, they won't be able to use the Ways." I took a deep breath and set my hand on his shoulder. "We'll be watching for your signal."

#

123

There was a chorus of music from the far side of the museum. I could pick out Dominus's fiddle, but also a drum, and a low brassy thing like a trumpet, but smoother. The music was an interesting weaving back and forth between the instruments, as though that was how they greeted each other. Three goblins moseyed down the aisle, stopping to examine some of the items as they came, with a cloud of masked people skittering around them holding their goblets or carrying their bags. Dominus was lecturing as he led them, their music fading into the background while they spoke. The instruments floated above them, but as the melody faded, they sank down into the waiting hands of their servants.

"I think you'll find this discovery particularly interesting," Dominus said, his voice bright and exacting. "I found this under some of the rubble of the tower. A genuine coral dagger, one of the few weapons of the Wild capable of piercing the followers of Ventor's divine armor."

"Expanding into weapons, Dominus? After denying my offers for trade so many times?" A woman goblin with piles of perfect blond curls above a delicate silver mask flashed her completely black eyes at him. She was in a long, white gown that shimmered different colors when she moved.

"My dear Heres, you know it's about the thrill of discovery, the study of the item." He pointed to the dagger. "But once I'm through learning about this one, I'm sure we'll have plenty to discuss about a possible trade, perhaps for that adorable little water sprite you keep in your fountain?"

"Not for a mere dagger," Heres said with a laugh.

"You've been pressing for trades for that thing for years, Dominus." This goblin was wider than the other two, but was dressed just as fine, in a long, purple tunic over white trousers. "She is never going to give it away."

"I think I have something that may change her mind," Dominus said, and I clenched my fists, the burning rising up in me again. "Or yours, Vinco, if you still have that serra—"

"You must have caught yourself something big to have such high ambitions," Vinco interrupted. "Why don't you take us straight to the prize."

"Very well, but you are missing some very fine items. This way." Dominus bowed and swept his arm in our direction, leading the group over to our glass-enclosed box of dirt. At first, the troupe did not look impressed, but as they drew closer, they perked up.

"What is that?" Heres asked, tapping her long nail on the glass. "Is that a Changeling?"

"Hardly worthy of your collection, Dominus," Vinco said. He barely looked at us before turning away and examining a different case. "Changelings are a dime a dozen and had nothing to do with the fall of the tower."

"Yes, yes, artifacts of the fall are a huge goal, but I think you will find something even more appealing about this one." Dominus placed his hand on the glass, opened the door, and joined us in the dome, bringing his fiddle in as well. "The glass cases will keep the magic from affecting them," he said to me. "We're going to doing a demonstration. A retelling of the fall of the North Tower." He swept his arms around as he announced, his cape swinging out behind him. "Just follow the narration, and make it look convincing, hm?"

I nodded, as though I understood exactly what he expected of me. He slipped my flute out of his sleeve and handed it to me. When he raised his fiddle to play, I brought up my flute. He counted out four beats, and we began.

He played a stately marching melody, and I caught onto it quickly, adding in flourishes where I thought they would sound appropriate. I cast an apologetic glance at Otsoa and Drinn before the song took hold of them, but I'm not sure if they noticed. The song grabbed them fast, and they lined up and marched to the tower. They marched around it several times, then stopped on either side of it as though they were sentries on duty. Then my flute and Dominus's fiddle leapt up into the air, and switched to a softer song, something Wild but cool and rhythmic, like the waves of the sea.

"When the foolish followers of the Breaker first came to our shores," Dominus began, gesturing to Drinn and Otsoa, "they constructed their stone tower and began weaving their magic, trying to fight off the Wild that lived here." Drinn and Otsoa began waving their hands, and purple-red waves of fire began dancing around the tower, wilting the trees nearby them. "We sent our pleas to our glorious Winter Queen to send aid, to no avail. She ignored our pleas and left us to fend for ourselves against the Iron Knights and elvish wizards."

Dominus swept into place in front of Drinn and Otsoa and mimicked throwing icy bolts at them and the tower. The frosty streams were melted immediately in the fall of flame around them. For the moment, I was not part of the story, and not under his attention. I looked toward the place in the dome where he opened the door, but still saw no seams or opening at all. The other two goblins were watching, their faces twisted into bitter grimaces.

"So we shook off our ancient bonds, denied our duties to one who neglected her duties to us, and summoned something that would rid us of the Breaker's servants forever." Dominus took hold of me then, forcing me to stand at the edge of the sea. He filled my mind with a massive, terrifying image, and I responded by recreating the image around me with my illusion song. Wings sprouted from my back, claws grew from my hands and feet, and a long lizard-like body spread out behind me. I stretched and stood yards above the heads of all the others in the form of a dragon. They had awakened a dragon? Any thoughts that they had been driven mad from living in this dark place for centuries disappeared. They had been mad long before that.

I rushed forward, and the sea moved with me, sweeping up and flooding around the tower, extinguishing the flames. Drinn and Otsoa climbed up the back side of the tower. From my now-higher vantage point, I could see that it was just a ladder with a false tower front built around it. They peered up at me through the open top, and a light began to glow from the tower, the usual beacon lit to call for help from other Wardens. They threw more fire at me from within the tower, and I fought back with the waves around me, and with spouts of slimy water from my dragon jaws. Chunks of the tower fell to the ground, but Drinn and Otsoa stood their ground, firing back with all they could.

"And then the Breaker's minions did something we did not expect." The light in the top of the tower flared, and then seemed to suck in on itself, before exploding out in a giant wave of flame that turned everything around it to the dry skeletal land we had seen before. The dragon illusion around me began to dissolve, and I collapsed into the sea, sputtering and straining as if in pain. "Everything Wild was thrown here, turned into the Wild that Was. The land was desiccated. It cost them dearly, but it cost us far worse." Drinn and Otsoa slumped over the edge of the tower's crown, and I went still and cold as driftwood.

Outside the dome, Vinco and Heres burst into somber applause. Dominus continued the song long enough to bring Drinn, Otsoa and I to the dome's side and make us bow to them.

"That was glorious, Dominus," Vinco said, taking a closer look at me. "She must be more Wild than not."

"I believe she is at least half. And trained in great Mosine's blessed arts. You see how real her illusions appear?" Dominus asked.

"Oh, Dominus, that would be worth trading quite a lot for," Heres said. She was almost bouncing up and down with excitement.

"Let's have a taste first," Vinco said. "I hate to be so finicky, but I would like proof that it works. You know nothing gets through the glass domes."

"Naturally. I would be glad to have a demonstration. But let's not tax her energies so much." He motioned at the masked creatures surrounding them. They all looked dejected, keeping their hungry eyes on me as they passed the case and left the museum to the goblins.

A wave of nausea hit me, and I turned my head to see Otsoa's reflection in the glass. He tilted his head just enough for me to notice, then closed his eyes. Drinn saw it too, and I saw her close her eyes as well. The minions would be out of the way, only three unsuspecting goblins, and we were wearing masks. This was our chance.

Once all the masked people had left, Dominus opened the door in the glass and motioned for me to follow him out. I hesitated, then dragged out every step I took just enough, trying to give Otsoa enough time to make his spell work. When my foot crossed the threshold, I closed my eyes, felt him gathering in the power of the spell, and it made me gasp. It was sunlight, the light coming from somewhere above us concentrated and focused into a brilliant beam. It blazed down through Otsoa and out as a blinding light that lit up the whole case and sent the goblins howling away from us.

I ripped my mask off and bolted out of the dome searching the floor for a sewer hole. Otsoa was right behind me, his mask off as well, and he beelined for a spot an aisle over. I changed direction and got to the grate at the same time as him. I fought to pull it from the floor and looked back to see if the goblins had recovered yet. Drinn had not run after us. Instead, she was standing over one of the goblins with a strange-looking knife.

"Drinn, what are you doing?" I shouldn't have yelled it, shouldn't have drawn the goblin's attention, but I had to say something.

"I'm getting what I came for," she said, and slashed at Dominus's face. He screamed, blindly trying to fend off what was attacking him, but it did no good. She pulled something from him, dripping red, and stepped over his now motionless body. She tossed her old mask aside and set his mask over her eyes. Instead of simply settling into place it started to change shape, matching the

127

smaller contours of her face, molding to her skin. I could no longer see Drinn's eyes. There were only completely black orbs like the goblin's.

Chapter Thirteen

The doors of the museum flew open and dozens of masked people flooded in and crouched down beside their fallen masters, wailing over Dominus's wound. Others threw themselves at Drinn with weapons drawn. Drinn held up a hand and they all froze in place.

"Sorry all, under new management. Now, first things first," Drinn said. Heres and Vinco were panicking, still feeling around blindly to get away from Drinn. With a flick of her hand, Drinn commanded the two minions with weapons to take hold of them, then grasped them by the hair and pulled their heads back before slitting their throats. Drinn sent the minions dragging their bodies out of the museum. The rest stood up straight and stiff, like tin soldiers, and turned as one to face Otsoa and me.

"Go!" Otsoa urged me, grabbing hold of the grate and sliding it out of the way. I couldn't pull my eyes away from Drinn. What was she doing? Why wasn't she coming with us, and why would she send the minions after us? Otsoa pulled at my arm, and I snapped out of my shock long enough to jump down into the drain. Otsoa jumped in after me, and slid the grate shut, then commanded it with some short dwarvish words. There was a brief glow, and when the masked minions reached it and tried to pull it up, it refused to budge.

"Glade, go!" Otsoa shoved me toward the nearest pipe opening. I let him instruct me, pushing me through and around various pipes and tunnels until I had completely lost any sense of direction. "All right, stop. Stop!" He had to yank on my arm before I complied.

I huddled against a damp curved wall to catch my breath. "Now what?" I asked. My breathing wasn't slowing at all. I tried to count to slow it down, the way I would for singing or music, but it wouldn't obey.

"Put your mask on. We're getting out of here."

"Underground? The pipes won't be over there." I looked around, but it was dark here, not outdoors-with-starlight-dark, but deep-in-the-dirt-dark, and I couldn't even make out his outline. "We'll be buried alive."

"All right, so we'll find a way topside, and leave from there."

"Right, and rabid crowds of goblin slaves will follow us out." I ran my hands over my uncontrolled cloud of hair. They were shaking. Otsoa found my arm and took my hands between his.

"Just try to breathe, Glade. We're going to get out of here. One step at a time." His voice was low, and so certain. A warm tingling moved through our bond into me, a cool, deep feeling that stilled the raging fire inside. I managed to get my breathing under control and gripped his hand tightly.

"Right. Right, first we get topside. We'll worry about the next step from there." He kept hold of one of my hands and pulled me after him through a few more twists and turns until we found a large grate that let in the grayish light from above. A smile spread over my face, and I tried to push past him to get out.

"Stay here a moment, I'll take a peek," he said, patting my arm before climbing up to the grate.

"Hey, did you ever learn the song for the Way in Glenn's church?"

There must have been no one very near on the street. He risked lifting the grate enough to take a look around. "That's an odd question to ask right now."

"I was just thinking, if I'm not able to open the Way for you, you might have to do that part yourself."

"I'd have to open this side first," he said, coming back down to me. "And I was a little busy when we went through it the first time." He set his hands on my shoulders and made eye contact again. "Why are you worrying about that now? Let's get topside and get out of this crazy world first, all right? Then we can worry about songs and Ways and whatever."

"Sure. Sure, let's get out of here."

He nodded, smiled, and then clambered back up to the grate. He checked again to be sure no one was around, then motioned me to follow him above ground. The street was empty, bordered by low walls on both sides, with a dead end in one direction and a small plaza in the other. There was a stone fountain in it with no water. Instead, it was a perch for dark, oily birds.

"All right, mask up," he said, and put the dark, leathery mask on. I pulled mine out as well, but before I could pull it on, something plowed into me, knocking me flat and sending my mask skittering across the stones of the street.

Otsoa leveled his hand and shouted, and a blast of wind rushed over me, knocking whatever it was off of me, and the creature yowled in surprise. I scrambled up and behind him, and finally saw my attacker, a huge, muscled human. He narrowed his eyes behind his mask, then clenched and unclenched his massive fists.

"Give her up, wizard. We don't want you."

"I'm sure you'll be so happy to let me walk out of here," Otsoa said. He kept his arms out, one pointed at the muscle, the other protecting me. He kept inching us back toward one of the walls. I was still shaking, and I had no idea what he thought he would do. We reached the wall and flattened against it. Other minions began to appear at both ends of the street, some marching together. There were so many of them. I could let Otsoa shift, claw our way out of the crowd, but there were so many. I scratched at the wall and dug my fingers into Otsoa's arm.

"You brought us such a rich gift, why wouldn't we let you go?" The man feinted an attack. Otsoa responded with another wind blast, but it only blustered around the man. He laughed. "And with weapons like that, what are we going to do to stop you?"

"I'd like to see you try." Otsoa slapped his hand against the wall, and I heard something like glass break. There was a flash of blue light, and a door appeared in the stone. Otsoa shoved us through it, and we tumbled into a courtyard filled with torn fabric and dusty crates. He kicked the door shut and it vanished. "Come on, through here."

I scrambled to my feet; half-dragged up as Otsoa stood. The huge man appeared over the edge of the wall, lifting himself up as easy as taking the stairs. Otsoa grunted and pulled me toward a massive stone house in the middle of the courtyard. The door of the building was barely hanging on by rusty hinges. We burst inside and ran up the first stairs we saw, a winding staircase up a tilting tower. We could hear the large man and others slamming through the room downstairs after us. The stairs ended in a small round room with walls that slowly narrowed until they formed a point at the top. The only way out of the room was a wide window across from the door.

With a grunted shout, Otsoa collapsed the staircase. Shouts of pain and fear echoed through the house as our pursuers fell in a shower of stones and rubble. "We need a way out," he shouted to me. "Before they find another way up. Find something I can use."

I started digging through the clutter in the room, stacks of old papers and random bits of clothing, but came up with nothing. He started rummaging through the drawers and closets.

I took a look out the window myself. We were several stories up, high enough that I would probably break a leg jumping down. The wall was crumbling and uneven all the way to the ground, and any ledges or window frames looked like they would fall away if a pigeon landed on them. Scores of minions were gathering in the courtyard below. I leaned out and looked up. We had no chance of reaching the roof, either.

"Maybe I can find some feathers. You can fly us out," I said and went back to digging, but I had little hope. I had lost my mask, and we were surrounded. I paused in my search, gripping onto a half-stuffed pillow to force back the tears that were threatening to spill out of me. There was no way I was getting out of this place.

"Ugh, what I wouldn't give for a pinch of bat wing," Otsoa moaned, slamming a drawer shut.

"Wait, I have an idea." I hopped up and ran to the window again. "Come here, you have to see this." It was a terrible though, but it was the best I could do. One of us was getting out of this place.

"What is it?" He joined me at the window.

"Look just up here," I said, leaning out the window again and pointing toward the edge of the roof above us.

"What am I looking for? How is a roof tile going to help us?" While he peered up and out of the window, I took a deep breath, and grabbed hold of the silver pendant at his throat.

"It won't. You have to run for it." I said. I pushed my anger through our bond. His eyes snapped back to me, and he grasped my wrist. I watched the calm and lightning-quick thoughts going through his mind, analyzing all our options. Then the thoughts faded away, replaced with a narrow, frantic look of an animal caught in a trap. He fought it, trying to keep hold of his logic.

"No, Glade. Don't do this. Please." He tried to push my hand away, but I held tight to the pendant and pushed harder.

"They'd only find me, again. They will always find me." I said. "They won't be able to catch you." I tore the necklace from him and then I shoved him out the window. Even in his right mind he would know his best chance would be to change on the way down. He transformed into a jaguar in the air, the change happening so fast I nearly missed it, an elegant shift from one form to another. He turned himself around, so he landed on all fours and took off running away from the tower without a glance back at me. A few masked people tried to get in his way, but he pounced on them, or swatted them aside with his claws and kept going like they were little more than bumps on the road. He'd make it, I was sure. He'd make it out and Josie would find a way to make him human again, and they would be fine. I tucked the necklace into my pocket.

There was a grunt from behind me as the hulking form of the muscled human who had knocked me down before materialized. I turned back to the window and kept my eyes on Otsoa until the big minion took hold of me and dragged me away from the window.

Everything would be fine.

Then the man's hands closed on me. I struggled, throwing my arms and legs out to make him fight for every step he took, dragging me out of the room. When we reached the doorway, he twisted sideways, banged me against the wall, and everything went dark.

#

I awoke hanging from a set of iron cuffs against a damp, rough wall, stripped down to my shirt and trousers. Dim, flickering light came from somewhere, around a corner in the cave, thought it wasn't enough to let me see much of my surroundings. The iron burned against my skin. A fully Wild creature would have had it worse, the iron sizzling through their skin in just a few hours. It would leave scars on me but wouldn't kill me. The wound on my head throbbed, and blood crusted the back of my neck. The places was musty and filthy, but in a different way than the sewers. There it had just been waste. Here, it was sweat and blood and despair.

I hung there for a long time, going in and out of consciousness, with no one and nothing coming by, at least not while I was aware. The rage that had taken hold of me in this realm didn't seem to be affecting me either, so I was probably being kept inside the city somewhere. The need for freedom would do something similar soon, driving me mad enough to agree to anything Drinn wanted if she would only let me go. I was sorry that Midsummer had already passed. The only other time I had been imprisoned like this, by my own brother, the call of the Summer Queen freed me. It was the most compelling call of all, more than Wild song or anything Dominus could play, and I would obey it any cost. There wouldn't be a call for almost a year.

Sometimes I searched through the earth for something living, some small plant or insect, on the ridiculous hope that I could convince it to help me. But there was nothing living here. Everything was solid stone and slime and empty cold. Even if I had found something, I wasn't in the Wild. The plants and creatures in the free world didn't obey the call anymore, just like the people. Trying to get them to listen required a lot of pushing, and it drove them mad. It would be as likely to hurt me as help.

Anything I would have kept on me, what little we had brought in with us, was gone. Though I could work some magic with my voice it was mostly illusions. I couldn't pick a lock that way. Otsoa was gone, the necklace was gone, I was truly alone.

So I waited. I started trying to pick out shapes in the deep darkness of the cave or cell or whatever I was tucked away in. There was a long crack in the wall right across from me, maybe other sets of shackles hanging down around it. How much of that was actually there or was only in my mind I couldn't tell, but it gave me something to focus on, and helped me stay conscious for longer before passing out again.

The next time I woke, I had enough energy to shake my shackles in frustration. I'd never figure out how to escape if I kept dozing off. The sound echoed through the small stone room and made something on the floor scuttle. I tried to pull my legs up, in case a rat or two had been waiting around for a nibble, but I didn't hear any more scrabbling. There was a long sigh, and then the rattling of chains.

"Who's there?" I whispered into the dark.

"Ah, so you haven't given up." Dominus's silk voice answered. "You have so much fire in you."

"I thought she'd killed you." I was surprised to hear relief in my voice. It also scratched, like my voice box was made of sandpaper.

"No. Nearly, but no." He groaned softly and he moved again. "Still can't sit up for long. Be thankful it's so dark. I'm not a pretty sight just now."

"So what happens now, she becomes one of you?"

Dominus laughed, a weak creaking laugh that faded out into a wheeze. "No, of course not. Can someone become like you by popping your luscious green eyes into their sockets?"

"That was unnecessarily specific," I said. "But she can use it, the way you did."

"Well, she doesn't have the finesse I do," he said, the pride in his voice overshadowed by how weak he was. "But basically, yes. I'm sure she'll get bored with it all eventually. There's only so long the excitement of exacting vengeance can last. Though I will say she has an awful lot of anger. I fear my minions will not fare so well as I. And you will be long dead before she exhausts all of it."

"And that bothers you, does it?" I tilted my head back, resting it on the stone behind me. Could Drinn really be that angry over my secret? Or was she also angry at the goblins for . . . something? I couldn't guess what would have made her angry enough to do all of this.

"A little. Does that surprise you? You are such a wonderful dancer. We haven't enjoyed that for so long."

I tried to imagine being confined to this dark world, away from real sun and living trees and the song of the forest. "What did you do, that they sentenced you to live here? Was it the masks? Or did you really do what we acted out up there?"

"No, no. The masks we found later to make living here bearable. We needed something to allow us to control minions so we could live the lifestyle we were accustomed to. We were thrown in here for the worst crime the Wild can commit."

"You broke a deal?" I whispered it. Living in the Wild was a game of escaping notice and being strong enough to fight off anything that decided you were interesting. It was possible to disobey a stronger Wild thing, but it was difficult and not always worth the effort. But breaking a deal was different. It was something deep-seated in all Wild things to stay bound by deals, the one thing that could be counted on between unequal parties.

"Yes, we broke a deal. Ten of us together made a deal with the Winter Queen to keep the sea dragon asleep. We broke the deal and were sent here."

"You broke a deal with the *Winter Queen*? You woke a *dragon*? And you're still alive?"

"If you can call this living."

"What is this place?" The rambling explanation I had gotten from Grinf was rolling through my mind, but it still didn't make any sense.

135

"We call it the Wild that Was. Everything that once was Wild in your realm is here now, in reverse. So all that was light is now dark, all that was living is now sharp like stone, even the seasons are reversed, though I doubt you could tell out there. The temperature doesn't change much now."

"And the Queen made this just for you?"

"The Queen is strong but she's not that strong. I don't think it was made on purpose. Something strange happened during the battle over that tower. Some overpowered wizard and a paladin together cast a spell at the sea dragon as it clawed up on the shore and boom! Wild that Was."

"Hm. I'll have to make a note in the histories." I paused to cough. "We thought you were exiled before that."

"I bet there are hundreds of songs about us. Mourning the loss of our beauty and grace from the world of the Wild." Again, he laughed and ended up coughing as well. "I won't ask you to sing one. You sound parched. What happened to your wizard friend?"

"He ran off."

"Good for him. Though you'd think he'd have known some way to take you with him. You were too good for him, though. Something smelled off about him."

"He's got a girl waiting for him. I couldn't let him waste time trying to get me out of here."

"No one waiting for you, sweetness?" His voice grew wistful. "Back before all of this, I think we could have—ah, but you never lived in the Wild, have you? Not really."

"No."

"Oh, there's a nerve. Mother or father?"

I didn't answer. He waited a while, then snorted.

"Oh, I see, I can tell you all about our past, but we don't get to know any of your secrets."

"That does seem to be the way she works." Drinn's voice grated after the whispering, dry words between Dominus and me. "Makes you think she likes you, has your back, and all that. But never tells you anything more than she has to."

#

"You're holding up well," Drinn said. "I thought you'd be completely unconscious by now." The edges of the gilded mask she wore glittered in the

136

faint scraps of firelight that reached us. Her eyes seemed like two dark holes in her head.

"Yah, I'm doing great. Best room in the house."

"I seemed to remember how much you hated going underground. Never wanted to take any jobs with caves or dungeons."

"To be fair, no one ever really wants a job in a dungeon," I croaked.

"And all that time, you were lying to me."

"I know you're not doing this because I lied to you." I leaned my head back on the stone wall if only to keep from looking into those dark pit eyes. "We lied all the time. We were con artists."

"But not to each other." Her voice was calm. "Never to each other."

I shook my head. It only wobbled a little. She jerked my chin down so I was looking into her eyes. Her control through the mask was not as smooth and easy as Dominus's. It felt much more like being jerked around by a fishhook on a line.

"Oh, you don't believe me? Name one time I lied to you. Hm? When we were caught in that stupid trap in Tiangi because I'd let our cover slip. No, you knew I'd done that, because I told you. Or when that oriad was on our tail by the South Tower because I'd taken it's gemheart? No, I told you that too."

"And what would you have done if you'd known?" I squeezed my eyes shut. "Told me everything was all right? Kept my secret from the Wardens and the Watch and the Registry? You'd have been gone in a heartbeat."

"Me? You're the one who left."

"Drinn, please, just tell me the truth. Why are you doing this?"

"Why? For the same reason you do." She leaned in close and grinned. "I like it." Her grip tightened on me, not in the focused, caressing way Dominus had gripped me, but a cold vice grip that slowly clamped down around me, making it hard to breathe.

"No." I tried to pull away, to yank my head from her control. She grunted and tightened her magical grip. I struggled harder and managed to drag my head free. Drinn smacked me across the face. My lip split, swelling up and throbbing with pain.

"Why do you always have to make things more difficult?" Her voice had tipped from fully controlled to mildly frenzied. "You could never let me enjoy things." She smacked me again, keeping my body rigid so my head snapped around. My neck strained and something twinged hard in my shoulder.

"Stop," I said, throwing every ounce of command magic I could into the word. Drinn's hand froze in the middle of another swing, and she spat curses at me while she pushed through the spell. "What about this am I supposed to be enjoying, again?"

A new flash of anger helped her push though my spell and finish the next slap, though it was clumsy, and she caught her hand on my teeth. She moved away, still cursing under her breath. Dominus chuckled from the ground.

"Go easy on her, it's her first time," he said.

"Silence, you! I'll get to you later," Drinn barked. Two sharp thuds echoed as she kicked him. His laugh drew into a wet cough, and he fell silent again.

"Well, he's not wrong." I couldn't help myself. I wanted to strike back at her, and the only weapon I had were my words. "You're pretty rough."

"I'll make sure I have plenty of time to practice." She clapped her hands, and several people scrabbled into the room. They forced water down my throat and shoved some musty nuts and moldy cheese into my mouth. I was hungry enough that I didn't care how gross it was; I gobbled it eagerly. They tried to do the same for Dominus, but he spat the water out, and muttered something in some other language.

"I don't want your pity," Dominus said, spitting again.

"Fine. Waste away then." Drinn clapped again and the minions disappeared, shadows against the firelight. She put her hand under my chin and raised my face to hers, giving up on the magical control for the time being. "But you I'll keep alive enough to practice on. A few more days should weaken you enough for that."

"You have no idea," Dominus mumbled. "You have no idea what kind of fire burns in her."

Drinn took a long, slow breath, and went on without addressing him. "We will dance, you and I," she said to me. "The way that I want. No more lies, no more cheats. And you will never walk away from me again." She dropped my chin and swept out of the cell. In the quiet that followed, I listened to Dominus's shallow breaths wheezing in the darkness, and blinked back tears.

"Wow, sweetness. You must have given her some taste."

"I've never given her anything. She didn't know. Well, not until yesterday." My words were shaking as I tried to hold back the sobs. Drinn had been my closest friend, my only friend, for a very long time. It had broken me to push her away all those years ago. But seeing her like this, driven by the same stupid overwhelming thrills that controlled me, was too much.

"She must have known. Why would she have gone to all this trouble, if she hadn't known at least a little taste?" He huffed and shifted on the floor. "She must have known about the masks, too."

"I swear, I never let her feel any of it." I had worked hard to keep her away from any Wild song, picking the jobs cautiously, distracting anything so it went after me instead of her.

"Well, she must have gotten it somewhere. She's got quite the desire for control. She has a deal with a Wild One. She brings them the artifact; she gets to spend some time as a goblin torturing the one that got away. Seems like a fair deal."

"Does it really matter at this point? She'll puppet me around to do what she wants until I get called away by the Queen. Or if we do manage to get out, then you'll puppet me around until you're tired of me and throw me out into the courtyard to get eaten alive by your sick little minions." I stopped pretending and started crying, slumping so that I was hanging from the wrist irons.

"Hush, darling. Please don't cry. You must know I think better of you than that." He scuffled around until he was sitting up again, though I heard him grunt in pain a few times trying to get there. Then he slid forward as far as his restraints would let him. "That was no mere puppetry. The dance we shared, that was both of us. You swept over me as much as I took over you." His voice grew dreamy. "I would never let you go, sweetness. I'd have made you mine forever."

I let the iron burn into my wrists, and the tears burn down my cheeks until finally, blessedly, I passed out again.

Chapter Fourteen

I woke leaning against the wall. I tried to pull away from the cold clamminess, but my legs and arms refused to move. I tried to draw from the sunlight inside me to warm my limbs, but the light was weak. My legs refused to hold me up; they had become numb stumps that banged around clumsily. I ended up staying against the wall, relieving the tension on my manacles so they wouldn't burn into my wrists. At least I could still feel my arms. I had to work my hands from side to side every few minutes to gain a little relief. Maybe I was starting to go a little mad, but I turned it into a song, a rhythm of jingling chains under my grunts and moans.

"Are you well?" Dominus's voice was less scratchy than it had been. He sat up, then stood. "That is not a pretty song."

I chuckled as well as I could with my parched throat. "I get inspired by what's around me."

"Fair enough." He yawned. "You're hurting, and hungry. I can't do too much about it. Drinn will be suspicious. But I'll do what I can." He began his own low rumbling song, and I felt the fire within me warm and grow. It spread through my limbs, a painful tingling at first, then a soothing heat. But it let me get my legs under me and take some pressure from my burning wrists. Then he stopped.

I hissed and pushed off the wall toward him, but I was too weak to do much more than wobble sideways. "Why did you stop?"

"I don't give away anything for free. I have some unanswered questions. I like to learn all I can about my treasures."

"And if I answer them, you'll sing more?" I said it too fast, but I didn't care. I was freezing, and starving, and I wanted anything he would give me.

"Of course, a fair exchange. We have a deal?" His words wrapped me in a familiar embrace, or more like a vice that fit snug. I knew the feeling well. It would be comfortable and right unless I tried to break the agreement, and then it would squeeze the breath out of me. I couldn't fathom how Dominus and the other goblins had survived breaking a deal. The thought of it made me nauseous.

140

"One question, one answer, one more minute of song." I said. "We have a deal."

"One question, with clarifications," he added. "But I promise I won't take advantage."

"Very well. Ask away."

"Is it your mother or father that is Wild?"

I was surprised he went back to that one. "Mother."

"Do you know her name?"

"She has many, the Golden One, Mother of Flowers, Flowing Nectar." I hated talking about her. But at least he couldn't stay on the topic for long. All I knew were her names. I wasn't even sure I knew what she looked like. I imagined she had glowing skin, like mine, and the same crazed straw-like hair. But there were many such creatures in the Wild, and in my nightmare memories there were many of them. And none ever paid me any attention.

"Ah, that explains a great deal," he mused. I wanted to shout at him that it didn't matter and that he owed me his song now. He drew out the pause, then sang for me, flooding me with warmth and life. Not enough, of course, but enough to keep me awake and to ignore the stinging of my wrists and the numbness that kept trying to reclaim my legs.

"And your father is human? A rather dashing one, I suppose, if he was able to seduce the Mother of Flowers."

"Yes, the great Tor Balladeer, bard of the bower, the most swoon-worthy bard ever to sing east of the Lumina." Dad I could go on about forever. It wasn't much to brag about, but he was certainly interesting, and much more involved than my mother had ever been. Another minute of low, humming song, and a little strength returned to my legs.

"Did he raise you then? Teach you how to fight the temptations of the Wild?"

I scoffed. "Hardly. I was raised by the midwife that helped birth me."

"Ah, but he did something kindly for you. Though you mock him, it's not without tenderness."

I frowned. He was deducing all this just from the sound of my voice. Unless he could see well enough in the dark to judge my reactions. "That's not a question."

"If he abandoned you as well, why do you care for him so much?"

141

"He got me an apprenticeship with one of the best bard masters." Something stirred in the bond, the agreement between us.

"I don't think that was quite it. Though that was important to you." His shackles jingled, coming closer to me. He was reaching his hand toward my face. "Something deeper than that. Did he help you cheat on your final test?"

I took a shaky breath. A deep ache started in my chest as I remembered back to my final exam. I shook my head, and turned my face away from him, and the bond began to tighten. It was going to force me to answer.

"Come now, you can tell me. No one here but me and the rats."

"I didn't cheat." I took another slow breath, then another, until they were no longer shaky. "The final exam for a bard is a performance. You invite everyone you can to watch the show, held in a temple of Mosine. Once the show is over, everyone parties through the night, and from the magic or from the party everyone passes out. Then in the morning, if you are found worthy, Mosine blesses you and gives you the gift of magic."

I clenched my eyes shut against the memory. It had been delightful, for the most part. Everyone I had come to know, my first real group of friends because I had learned how to hide what I was, all gathering around to celebrate my graduation.

"Show me." He started humming, the tune he had used to make the reenactment show for his goblin friends.

"Please don't, I don't want to talk about this." The bond tightened further, pressing around my lungs as though I were wrapped in chains. I let the memory pour out of me, riding his song to create a glowing miniature between us. A miniature shrine to Mosine, decked in flowers. My classmates spread out around me, playing music or drinking or laughing. My father, and my teacher, and Josie sitting before the shrine.

"Looks delightful," Dominus said. "What went wrong?"

"My illusion failed," I said, then gasped for air as the bond loosened. In the miniature, the little figures began lying down and falling asleep. Time lapsed over the scene, growing dark and then light as the sun rose. But instead of my little Glade image, it was me in full Wild form. She woke and stretched, and then cried out in surprise at her appearance. My father woke next, and hurriedly threw his cloak around me to hide me from the others. There was only one other figure awake, one that had fallen asleep close by the shrine. He was staring at the figure of me.

"By morning I looked like this, Wild as the mountain thyme. Most of the crowd wasn't awake, yet. But Sam was. I . . . Sam was . . . I was in love with Sam." My cheeks flushed when I said it. All those years later. Then my heart twisted, remembering the look on his face when he saw me. The complete disgust. "He saw me. And he hated me. And dad made him forget."

"Made him forget?" Dominus gave me a longer dose of his song, suddenly much more interested in my stupid tale. The pain in my wrists faded, though my heartache remained. "Your father knows how to do that?" The miniature of my father reached out and touched Sam's head. Sam collapsed to the ground, and my father and I ran away from the scene. It faded away.

I shrugged. "That's the only time I saw him do it. I didn't ask him about it ever. I didn't want to know, and he didn't want to tell."

"Oh, so he never taught you that trick? Pity. That would be very convenient right now."

"No," I muttered. I was sobbing without sound, without tears. I didn't have any left in me. But the ache in my chest bloomed, filling me with the certainty that no matter what, no one would ever accept what I was.

"So that's why you keep Drinn at a distance. Why you keep everyone at a distance. You expect them all to leave, eventually."

"They always do." My words were barely above a whisper.

"And there it is." Dominus's voice was icy. I was too empty to care. "Was that really so hard?"

I didn't answer. There was nothing more I wanted to say, nothing worse I could have said. Of all the laws I'd broken, keeping myself disguised or conning with Drinn, the thing I regretted the most was that one night I'd let my father alter the mind of someone I loved.

Dominus backed away again and sang enough that I could feel my toes again. My shoes were damp, and my throat was still dry as sand, but I could stand up without swaying. Everything inside me had gone cold, and not even his song could stir me. I just let Dominus drone on.

"That's because they don't understand you. They never will. I know you think you've chosen the high path, the better path, sticking it out with these humans and elves and what not. But not one of them will ever accept you." He chuckled. "Not like I would."

Sure. Accept me as a pet, as a part of his exhibit. But maybe he was right. It was better than being punished for lying, and then treated as disgusting

143

when I finally showed what I was. I peered through the darkness at Dominus, paying closer attention to his words.

"But you're right, living in the Wild can be such a harrowing time. If you don't get the right Archon to take care of you, you could end up little better than a lap dog. Or a slave. And don't even get me started on the politics." He drew out the vowels in the word and groaned. "Always jockeying for position, trying to stand out enough to be loved by your caretaker but not so much that you pose a threat. I lived like that for centuries, Glade. You deserve better than that. Stay here with me."

I scoffed. "You say that like I have a choice."

"Of course you do. We do." There was another round of jangling chains, and then he stepped across the cave, putting one hand on the wall by my waist and the other on my cheek. "We can get out of here whenever we want."

A chill ran through me, and I shrank back against the wall and turned my face away from his hand. "If you were free why haven't you left already?"

"And leave such a treasure here? Never." He backed away a step. "Besides, I cannot get my mask back on my own. Magic like that is complicated. There are a lot of rules."

"You aren't allowed to kill her."

"That is one of them, yes."

I nodded but didn't ask anything further. I didn't care about the rules, I didn't care about getting out even. I just wanted to waste away already. That was what I deserved. Not to be forgiven, again, by Josie or Otsoa, not to be taken in by some benefactor in the Wild. Just to hang here and dry up like an old leaf.

Dominus cleared his throat. "That is why she hasn't disposed of me. But if you could incapacitate her, I could get the mask back and we could escape."

"Incapacitate, hm? You're not asking me to dispose of her?"

"I leave that up to your discretion. She has been rather hard on you." He leaned against the wall beside me. "What happened between you two? Is she really only angry because you lied to her?"

"I don't know what she's so angry about. There was a time when we only had each other to rely on, and she knew I was keeping a secret, but I didn't think she knew what it was. We were on a job, and I knew the Wardens we were guiding would get hurt if I didn't intervene, but I couldn't tell her how or why I knew." My words faded off into whimpering.

"Perhaps you should ask her a few questions before you incapacitate her."

"And just how am I supposed to do that? You've given me some energy, but she has your mask."

"That's right. She does." His tone dropped a few degrees, until it was a low purr. "I'll get her distracted, and I'll make sure you have the strength to do what you have to do."

#

"Time to wake up."

I peeled my eyes open to find Drinn towering over me. There was more light in the room now. Two torches were stuck in crevices in the wall behind her and I got my first real look at the hole she'd stuck me in. It wasn't much more than a wide crack in the rock with rows of shackles nailed to the wall, just far enough from each other to keep prisoners from touching. The light stung my eyes, so I squinted up at her. I had slumped against the wall again, dozing, but I didn't stand as she came closer. I didn't want her to know I was feeling better.

"I think we're ready for another try," Drinn said. She grabbed the hair on the top of my head and pulled it back, so I was looking straight up, and she peered into my eyes, pulling the eyelids down with her other hand. "You look about done."

She released my head and I let it flop down. Dominus was lying against the wall, his dark eyes unblinking, staring up at the ceiling. His face was a mass of red raw flesh around his eyes and down his cheeks where his mask had been. I couldn't tell if he was breathing. Then, very slowly, he closed and opened one eye, winking at me. I swallowed hard, and then Drinn pulled my head up again and shoved a leathery mask on my face.

"Stand up," she commanded, and my body obeyed. Pain jolted through my legs as I put pressure on them, but I only had pins and needles in my feet. She was getting better at controlling me. Instead of being yanked around by fishing lines, it felt more like jolts to my muscles.

She raised her hand to hit me, but stopped, her arm poised by her head. "What, no protest? No fighting back? No snide comments? You must be growing weary."

She tilted my head, so I was looking at her, but I stared straight through her. That would sometimes work to keep bullies from attacking. She growled

145

and knocked my head back against the wall. I had to blink stars out of my eyes before I could see her grimacing face again.

"I never did make it into a guild, you know." Drinn put me through the motions of covering my mouth in shock. "I know, I know, I was so close. Certainly had the skills. I just never could afford the right equipment. And once word got around that we'd led those Wardens to their deaths, well, that didn't help my reputation."

A twinge fired in my head, and she forced me to speak. The words came out strained, and my voice sounded like my mouth was full of marbles. "That is not what happened," she made me say.

"Oh, I know that, and you know that. But no one else believed me. And then, of course, there were the sirens."

She didn't have to force me to speak then. "Oh, no, Drinn." The day we had parted ways, we had led a group of Wardens to what we thought was an easy job. But I had known there was something stronger, something more dangerous waiting for them. I had known right away they were creatures of Winter. I went back to warn the Wardens, and Drinn had left, refusing to help. The sirens took control of me and killed the Wardens. I thought she had been well and gone before the sirens had attacked.

She didn't have to force me to speak then. "Oh, no, Drinn." I thought she had been well and gone before the sirens had arrived to attack the Wardens, and me.

"They found me before they reached the Wardens. Took me along with them for the fun. Something about how good I am with knives." She spread my arms as wide as they would go, stretching me to the limit until I winced, but she had closed my mouth and I couldn't cry out. "So once we were done with the Wardens they decided to keep me around for a while. Just for fun. Do you know how lovely that was, Glade? Being the particular pet of a set of sirens?"

She pushed my hands up to my face, covering my eyes and making me shake like I was sobbing. My head bowed, and I tried to get a look at Dominus, but my fingers were stiff and close against my face. He was supposed to be providing a distraction. What was he waiting for?

"I won't bore you with all the twisted details of what I've been through since then. But I will let you know; I've tasted all kinds of Wild song. And you know what?" She tilted my head up so she could whisper in my ear. "I think I like the sirens better."

She pushed through my mind again and forced words out of my mouth, though if she had let me go, I would have said them anyway. "I am so sorry, Drinn."

She looked me over, her chin up, her shiny eyes narrowed, and shook her head. "I don't believe you." With a swat of her hand, she banged my head against the wall and everything went dark.

The light returned slowly, and my vision remained blurred. Drinn had turned away from me and was staring down at Dominus, grimacing like she had found him stuck to the bottom of her shoe. He was lying perfectly still, staring off at nothing.

"The Wild has so many rules," Drinn said. I couldn't tell if she was speaking to me or to Dominus. She still had control of my body and was holding me at rigid attention. "He can't kill me to get the mask back. I can't kill him to keep it." She turned her head and smirked at me. "So, if you are truly sorry, if you want to prove to me that you regret what you let happen to me, you kill him."

I blinked to clear my vision and wondered if I was having some kind of bad dream or hallucination, but she was still staring at me expectantly. I laughed, a weak huff, and tried to shake my head.

"I can't kill him. He's far too strong." He was fully Wild, and much older than I. There would be no chance, in this bedraggled state, that I could even hurt him.

"Without his mask he's weak as a kitten." She kicked him to make her point, and his body flopped like a rag doll. "But then, I guess I would understand if you choose him over me. You did choose him over Otsoa, and he was much more your friend than I ever was. Does he know what you are?"

"That's not what happened," I croaked. "I wanted him to be safe. That was all I ever wanted for you too." But the guilt of it all stung, and I couldn't make the words sound believable, even to me.

"And that worked out so well. And now Otsoa is lost to his wild nature, and I've been taken in by Winter. You've left quite an impressive wake, Glade." She leaned against the wall beside me, and I felt her pushing for the light inside me to fade. Could she control my feelings as well as my actions? Dominus had affected my Wild magic but hadn't made me feel anything.

Though his control had been so much more subtle and smooth than what Drinn was doing to me now. Would I have noticed if he had made me feel what he chose?

"I can't, Drinn. I can't kill him. I won't."

"You owe me," she said, and she pressed harder against the fire inside me. As an instrument of Winter, she must have learned how to suppress the magic of Summer. As the light faded, I felt my limbs grow cold, and my mind began to feel numb. The image of stabbing Dominus with one of Drinn's knives appeared in my head. I shook it off, wondering where that had come from. Another replaced it, the thought of tossing him into the sea.

"Drinn, please," I groaned between clenched teeth. This was worse than all the beatings she or Dominus could have given me. She was taking away my light. Thoughts of killing whoever I needed to, Dominus, the little minions, anyone, in order to escape no longer seemed as harsh or frightening.

A low humming filled my ears, and I let it wash over and through me. The Summer fire inside me glowed to life and burned away the fog in my mind.

"Silence you slug," Drinn said, and she kicked Dominus again. He didn't flinch but kept humming his warming song.

"Make me," he hissed between clenched teeth. She kicked him again, and he grinned. The flames inside me rose to a bonfire. This was a different kind of madness. Rather than the cold calculation Drinn had tried to force on me, this was all Wild abandon. Who cared if anyone got hurt? I just needed to sing and let the fire take over me. I choked it back, trying to hold on to my mind, to stay balanced between freezing and burning. I didn't want to kill either of them, but the thought that ached the most was that they were both trying to use me to kill the other. It wasn't about them choosing me as their friend or companion, or any kind of caring about me at all. I was a tool, pure and simple. They may as well have been struggling over a knife.

"Stop!" I threw every ounce of strength I had into the word; every bit of magic I had learned as a bard and every bit of Wild fire went into that one command. They froze, locked into their hateful stare. Dominus had stopped humming, but the Wild song inside me was still threatening to take over. It was going to flood me eventually, but I was going to do everything I could to direct it before it did.

I couldn't control them with my mind, not the way that cursed mask allowed them to do. But I had them under the spell of my voice, at least for now. I looked around the cave desperate for what to do next.

"Set me free," I told Drinn. Her gleeful grin fell into a long frown, but she pulled a set of keys from her belt and unlocked the chains on my wrists and ankles. I sank to the ground and sighed in relief. "Good. Now take off the mask."

She resisted, straining against the command, holding her arms rigid against her sides. Dominus twitched beside me, trying to break free from the spell as well. I glared at him, and he grinned back. I could see the reflection of the light from my brilliant green eyes in his dull black ones.

"Take it off," I ordered again. Drinn strained against me but raised her arms to her face and pulled off the mask. I reached up and she passed it down to me, gasping when I took it in my hands like she was coming up for air after being pulled into the ocean. It didn't feel any different to me than the flimsy mask I had on. With one swift motion I crumpled it in my hands and tore it apart.

Dominus screamed and started shaking so violently that he banged against the wall. Drinn cursed at me and lunged down, just as Dominus threw himself toward me. Both were free of my spell now, and the curse of the mask, but I didn't care. My Wild song filled my ears, my heart raced as the light within grew to a raging blaze. I allowed myself to be overcome by the fire within me and blacked out.

Chapter Fifteen

Waking this time felt like clawing my way through a pile of sand. Every part of me was itching and dry, my throat was so parched I could barely screech out a sound, and my muscles protested every attempt to move. I wondered if I had finally dried up like a fall leaf and this was my new existence until I became dust and blew away. Then I felt the flickering torchlight on my eyelids, and heard tiny scuffling feet nearby, and I knew I was still in that hole of a dungeon.

I blinked my eyes open and watched the faint torchlight make the shadows flicker over the ceiling. The scuffling sounds grew louder. They were too large to be bugs or rats crawling nearby. A harsh whisper drifted to me from the cave beyond the crevice I was tucked into.

"No, I'm not going back in there until she calls," the whisperer said. "I'm still feeling the slap from last time I tried to anticipate what she wanted."

"But she's been quiet so long," answered another voice, this one softer and younger.

"We should count it a blessing and go on about our business. The less we have to serve her, the better."

"I'm telling you, there is something different this time. It's too quiet."

"Well you go in there, then," the first voice rose, but hushed again right away. "But don't say I didn't warn you."

The whispers stopped and the shuffling footsteps picked up again, getting closer. I raised myself up on one arm and peered through the shadows around me. Dominus was still huddled against the wall, but his face was turned away from me, and he looked more like a pile of cloth wrapped around sticks than his former lithe self. Further back in the crevice, Drinn had collapsed against the wall, one arm draped over her eyes.

I tugged at Dominus's shoulder. His body flapped back toward me and then cracked and crumbled, like he'd been made of dry clay. I lunged away from him toward Drinn.

"Drinn?" I hissed. "Drinn, come on, we have to go." I slid her arm away from her face, and it fell to her side. "No, Drinn, please." I grabbed her shoulder and tried to shake her awake. When the light fell on her face, I saw

150

burn scars across her cheeks, left by Dominus's mask I supposed, and her eyes were gone. I recoiled and covered my face. I didn't want to think about this now, I had to get away, but the thought kept intruding back into my mind. She's dead. Dead and gone. And it was my fault.

I sat there until the pain dissolved into a numb ache. Whatever happened to them could have been because they were trying to kill each other. But I had a pit in my stomach that echoed it was my fault for destroying the mask.

"Mistress?" A cautious whisper sounded near the entrance. My heart jumped into my throat, and I scrabbled around for something to cover myself. I shoved the panic aside and did the first thing that came into my head. I couldn't make a permanent disguise without my makeup, but I could make something that would work for an hour or so. It would have to be enough. I hummed Dominus's song under my breath and concentrated on the shape of that ornate mask and his completely black eyes.

"Mistress?" I echoed, rising to my feet with as much grace as I could muster. Imitating his voice was difficult. I couldn't quite make it as smooth as his, but he had been locked in here as long as I had. I hoped that would be enough excuse to sound like a scratchy-throated version of his silky voice.

The masked halfling in the opening of the crevice gasped, but it was a sound of relief and joy. "Master! Oh, master you are still alive!" She rushed forward and would have hugged me, but I stopped her with a hand gesture. My illusions only fooled the eyes, and if she touched me, she'd know I wasn't her master. She stood looking up at me with big shining eyes, her hands clasped in front of her.

"I am. But I am weary. Gather the others. Tell them to prepare a tray of food for me to be set outside my chambers. I am not to be disturbed."

"Of course, Master! We are so glad you are alive! That pretender was so terrible!"

"And so she has paid for her crimes," I said, and swept my hand to indicate Drinn's body. My stomach lurched, and I held my breath to keep down a sob. "Now, I will rest. Go and do as I command."

"Yes, Master, right away Master." She didn't pay any attention to the pile of ashes that had been Dominus, instead rushing out of the crevice and telling her companion the joyous news. The whispers gave way to shouts bubbling over with happiness and what they would do to celebrate now that their proper master was back.

I fell to my knees, fighting back nausea and the deep sobs that wanted to break through my shaky control. Rather than give in, I started going over scales in my mind, imagining my fingers running over my guitar with each rise in the notes, until my breathing was back to a regular rhythm, and I could stand without wanting to vomit. With slow, deliberate movements, I climbed out of the caves. I followed the rows of torches in the direction the whisperers had gone, stumbling over rough-hewn steps in the stone, and then emerged into the brilliant light of Dominus's hall.

Ignoring the stares from any servants I passed, I found my way to a side door and out into a garden grown over with mold. The strange twilight of the Wild that Was was so welcoming I just stood there a moment, my face turned up to the darkened sun, and breathed in the thick musty air. It was painful walking away from that place. I should have buried Drinn. I pushed through a broken gate and out into the city. The masked people around me kept their heads down and kept their distance, probably happy to not gain the notice of a goblin out for a stroll, but their presence made my skin crawl. Could we have freed them, Otsoa and I, if hadn't sent him away? He was out there somewhere, stuck in his jaguar form, also my fault. With a shiver, I shrugged all the questions away and kept walking.

I wound my way back to the trash heap. One lone, masked person was picking through the garbage, dressed in the worst set of rags I had seen in this place. They were deathly thin, their cheeks hollow and their eyes bulging behind the grisly mask. They froze when they saw me, dropping their head and curling in on themselves to appear smaller. I was too tired to be truly angry. Instead, a cold, unsympathetic thought ran through my head. *How pathetic*, I thought. *How sad.*

"Come here," I commanded them. They obeyed, hurrying to cower before me. "Give me your mask."

I could see now it was a young girl. She turned her face up to me contorted in shock and horror. Her hands shook as she wrung them in front of her in a begging gesture.

"What did you say, master?" Her voice was tiny, just a whisper of fear.

"Give me your mask."

"But how will I obey?" She asked, then even softer. "How will I be fed?"

152

"I will take you with me. Away from this place and feed you the most delightful things." I wasn't really lying. I could take her with me, set her free from this garbage heap and feed her all the Wild song she liked. That was not a better choice for her in the long run, but I could get her help back in the real world. "But you must give me the mask."

"Please, master, don't ask that of me." She groveled lower. "I will do anything else you ask. Just not that."

I grabbed her by the ragged front of her shirt and ripped the mask from her face. "Away with you. Find another trash heap to sleep in. Go on!" My shouts chased her away from the place, but the sounds of her sobs echoed in my ears. I wove through the garbage to the wall we had entered through.

With a long sigh, I raised my hand to knock, but the wall swung away before I touched it. I rushed out, letting the wall swing shut behind me. I gripped the mask in my hand and blinked back to the real world.

Long rays of sunlight fell on my skin. The salty air tickled my nose, and the sound of the sea caressed my ears. I dropped the mask, and trampled on it until it was ground into the sandy earth.

Then I was bowled over by a large cat roaring so loud it vibrated through my chest. We landed on a patch of gravel, the jaguar's paws on my shoulders, his teeth an inch from my face.

"Otsoa! It's me! Wait!" I released my illusion, turning back into my true form, glowing eyes and all. Otsoa panted against my cheek and roared again, then paused. He lowered his nose to my throat and started sniffing. My breath caught. With a snort, he backed off of me and let out a strange yowl, then thumped against me as I sat up and threw my arms around him.

"You idiot," I said into his fur. "You were supposed to get somewhere safe."

He yowled again and tilted his head to stare at me. It was so much like one of his human expressions, the one that asked, 'what were you thinking?' when I did something foolish.

"Very well. Just let me breathe a minute, and we can be on our way."

He took a slow walk around me and sniffed the air.

"No, Drinn didn't make it," I said around a large lump in my throat.

He planted himself at my back and let me lean on him. I didn't doze off this time. I just sat, soaking up the true sunlight and breathing in the fresh air for a time before heaving to my feet and heading back to the entrance to the Way.

I hesitated at the spot where I could feel the Way humming. The remains of our camp were nearby; nothing more than a small pile of cold ashes from the fire Drinn had made. Scrubby bushes waved in the sea breeze; the mountains loomed to the north. It looked like nothing had changed. But Drinn was dead. Shouldn't that have changed something?

Dread filled me. I was about to step through to a temple in the middle of the largest city in Drakir, with no disguise or even a hood to cover my face. But Otsoa would not let me wait. He bumped several times against the backs of my legs until I swatted at his nose.

"All right, all right. Let's do this then." I supposed I could appeal to Roya to get me out of whatever bind awaited me on the other side. But technically I wasn't doing this job for Roya. I was working for Negri, and I had no idea if he would even own up to that, let alone deal with any consequences. Especially since I was not bringing anything back with me.

I opened our side first, singing a song of loneliness and the sea. Then I opened the other with a hymn of sunshine and searing strength. I braced myself. The portal swirled open. And nothing happened. No guards jumped through to arrest me. No confused clerics rushed to see what had opened in their offices. Just silence and the brightness of the inside of the Temple of Solis greeted us. So we stepped through.

"Ah, there you are." A calm voice said. A tall, thin man was standing to my left, dressed in the red robes of Roya's household, though he was a good deal younger than Roya. "I am glad you have returned. Are you injured? Do you require healing?"

"Probably," I croaked at him. "Who are you?"

"I am one of Roya's assistants. When you stopped communicating, we thought to follow you to the North Tower, and Glenn let us know about your travel plans. Since I could not follow you through there," he waved at the portal. "I thought it best to await your return here for a day or so more before sending a party north."

I nodded, happy that someone was expecting my return, but not sure what to say to the frightening efficiency of it all. At least I didn't have to face Negri himself right away.

The assistant was trying not to stare at me. I had seen that look many times in my childhood. But then his eyes landed on Otsoa, and he frowned.

"If you will come with me, we have a coach waiting. I was also given a cloak for you, though he had not warned me . . . well . . . I hadn't known what it was for." He turned and lifted a large red cloak from the table beside him and held it out to me. "I will take you to Cyfar, and you can rest up before giving a report." He looked down at Otsoa again. "Is it tame?"

I huffed. "More tame than I am." I pulled the cloak around me and pulled the hood up so it concealed my face. Then I followed him out into the alley between temples and climbed into the cushioned coach.

I slept most of the way back to Cyfar, a still, undreaming sleep that left me stiff and a bit nauseous when I woke. We transferred to a boat when we reached the city and were taken up to the second level, to a comfortable inn. The assistant, who never told me his name, healed me with magic. He had thick soup and honey water brought to me, and he told me to eat up and rest for a while longer. He made sure Otsoa was comfortable too, though I have no idea what inn in Cyfar accepted jaguars as guests.

I slept a little more, but the dread of the coming meeting was catching up to me, and I wanted to get it over with. The assistant was seated just outside my door, so I knocked and let him know I was ready to go.

Visiting Roya's palazzo always made me feel small and shabby. The pristine columns and lush gardens all whispered of wealth and status and made my worn leather armor and faded tunic look beggarly. Instead of his office, we were led to a large, round parlor. It was open to the sky above, had a fountain in the middle, and had piles of cushions on long, silk-covered chairs.

I sank into one of the chairs, sending pillows toppling to the floor. Before I could pick them up, Otsoa flopped down onto them and wriggled, then set his head on his paws.

"I wonder if this is where he fires everyone, or if this is extra special treatment for us," I said. Otsoa lolled his tongue out at me and gurgled something like a laugh.

We waited a long time. I had never known Roya to be late, and he wasn't the sort to make people wait out of some weird sense of power. If that had been his goal, he wouldn't have buried us in pillows, he would have us standing in his office until he arrived to ask us to sit in the hard, high-backed chairs. At last, he blustered into the room and took up a stance by the fountain, facing us. His red robes were wrinkled and dirty along the bottom, and he wore no hat. He took a few deep breaths, then waved his hand at me.

"I apologize for being late. It was unavoidable, I'm afraid." His cheeks were flushed, and his voice was breathy. I had never seen him so out of sorts. "I hope you are well." He looked down at Otsoa and raised an eyebrow. He was beginning to calm down. "I was sorry to hear of your predicament," he said to the cat.

"I thought it would be better than the alternative," I said. Otsoa looked up at me, and I thought I saw a glimmer of understanding there, though it may have been wishful thinking. "I'm well enough," I said. "Tired, but I'm fine. Your assistant did some things to help my healing."

"You are fortunate to have returned at all." He flattened his lips, as though realizing how doomful that might have sounded, then smiled. "It is good to see you back, and in one piece."

"Thank you."

"Drinn is . . .?"

I lowered my head and nodded.

He cleared his throat. "I am sorry. Will you be alright speaking of this now? We can hold off on the official report."

"I'd rather get this over with," I muttered.

He made a small bow to me, then moved to a shelf along one wall and brought down a stack of papers and a long red quill. When he set them up on the side table, the quill stood up on its own.

"Please," he said waving toward the quill. "Begin whenever you are ready." Part of me was relieved, but I was also confused. I didn't want to end up losing any benefits from my contract just from missing an important detail like reporting back to the person who had actually hired me.

"Is Negri not joining us? Will this count legally as my official report?" The quill started scratching out my words as I spoke.

Roya sighed, then sat down on a padded footstool next to Otsoa. "Negri has disappeared." He looked at me directly when he said it, as though it was a regular occurrence. I wasn't sure what to say to that. I knew very little about Negri but had guessed he was who Roya used for less-than-legal jobs. Everything he'd hired me for previously were jobs that no one would care much about other than people like Otsoa and me, caught up in things we shouldn't have been. But they had all been strictly legal and official.

"Did you know?" I asked finally. "Did you know what he was asking us to do? What he wanted us to find?"

"Do you?" he countered. "I believe he only made Drinn aware of what your true target was."

"I know what Drinn was trying to take. Whether that was what Negri had tasked her with . . ." I shrugged. Just saying her name made my throat swell up. I swallowed hard. "Did he know what it would be like? What the goblins can do? They had a kind of Wild magic I have never seen before."

"Glade, please calm yourself. Would you like something to drink?"

"No! I want to know if you understood what he was sending us into."

"I had no idea. I would not have allowed him to hire you if I had known." I had never heard him speak so softly, his low voice barely a rumble.

I leaned back into the cushions and took a few long breaths. Then I launched into my report. This wasn't a fun version of events, just a boring retelling of the bare facts of the story, starting with the discovery of Drinn's bit of leather that let her jump into the Wild that Was, finding the Ways by breaking into the temple, learning what the masks really did and what the Goblins could do. When I was done, I had to wipe tears from my cheeks. Roya moved and I thought he was going to take my hand. Instead, he collected the pen and papers, rolled them up and tucked them away in his sleeve.

"You will receive whatever minimum payment Negri promised you for the job, as well as any compensation I can for your recovery."

I shook my head. "I don't care about the money, Roya. Will you fulfill what you promised for Glenn?"

"Of course. That is another reason for the delay today. We think we have located Ura." He held out his hand as I sat forward. "Do not get too excited. It is only a possible lead. As for this other issue," he said, looking down at Otsoa. I didn't let him finish.

"I don't think I can do this anymore," I blurted. The ache in my chest eased, and I realized I had been hoping that he was going to fire me. I was hoping I would never have to do another crazy job for him again, even if it meant working double shifts at Potions and Powders the rest of my life. He frowned, a pained look in his eyes.

"What do you mean?"

"I don't think I can work for you anymore. It's too much. It's just too much." Otsoa hopped up onto the seat beside me and I leaned against him. I only just managed not to start sobbing. Roya was silent for a long time, watching me closely. I'm not sure what he would have done if I had burst out in tears. He seemed torn between joining me on the couch and running away.

"You do not have a choice," he said at last. "You work for me, or I will ensure you cannot work at all."

I couldn't meet his eyes. Roya was a good boss. And we had done some good in the world. And I'd nearly died every time. But now I had ruined the job and killed my own fellow adventurer. I couldn't go on.

"Please. I will only fail you again."

"You did not fail," he said. "You just paid more than you were willing. I cannot simply let you go. There is more for you to do." He crouched down beside me and held out a folded sheet of paper. "Take this. For our friend, here." He nodded toward Otsoa. "And I will be in touch about your payment, and your next assignment."

I took the paper, thanked him, and shoved Otsoa so he jumped down from the couch, and we made our way out of the piazza.

#

This was not my first failed mission. Most Wardens had at least one or two good stories about the one 'that got away,' or, 'that time at the tower when I almost didn't survive.' But this was different. I could have taken what Negri wanted, what I assume he wanted, and brought back that vile mask to him. Instead, I had crushed the treasure I had sought, lost hold of one companion's mind, sentencing him to life as an animal, and killed the other.

I returned to the Branch and Vine, cowering like a beaten puppy. I didn't go in right away, waiting to see if there were many guests going in or out, or any signs that there was an event going on. When a baker arrived carrying baskets of bread, I peeked through the door after him, and Josie spotted me. She blew past the baker and out the door to Otsoa and me, well, mostly to Otsoa, who let her hug him tight. Then she looked up at me, noticed I was only disguised by a droopy dark cloak, and dragged us in. There was no event going on currently, but she let us know there would be one soon, so she wasn't able to keep us downstairs. She tucked us away in an upstairs room, and promised she'd be back.

Josie brought dinner up to us that night, and Glenn arrived. He looked weary, but he fussed over me all the same, checking me for wounds and adding his own healing spells, mumbling that the assistant had done only the bare minimum for me. His healing spells were better by far, much more familiar and comforting, than anything the assistant had done.

We sat around the small table in my room, Otsoa leaning against Josie's legs, Glenn asking if I needed anything else every so many minutes. I ignored him.

"I'm going to fix this," I said, staring down at Otsoa. Josie licked her lips and shook her head.

"Glade, don't."

"No, no arguments. It's my fault, and I'm going to fix this." I stabbed at the leafy greens on my plate for emphasis. Otsoa yowled and put his large paw on my knee.

"I'd rather you didn't."

I stared across the table at her. They had been planning so much. They thought they would have more time together, and I had robbed them of that. "I have to try."

"No, you really don't. Every time you do, you make things worse. It's not your job to try and fix everything. You need to stop trying."

"There are a lot more things wrong with this world than I thought," I said. "And I already thought it was pretty messed up. And I never thought I could fix any of them. I wouldn't even know where to start. But this, this I can try to fix. So no arguing." I moved my hand to Otsoa's paw. "Somehow, we'll figure this out."

He rested his chin on my hand, his large golden eyes staring up at me. I meant it. I unfolded the paper Roya had given me, flattening it on the table. The others peered at it, and Otsoa tried to peek up over the table to look as well, though I had no idea if he could read when he was in this shape.

"Is that Old Human?" Josie turned the paper sideways, then turned it around completely the other way. "I never could tell which way was up with those weird, blocky letters."

"It is. It's a legend from pretty far back. Supposedly from near when the humans first came to Drakir. Roya got it translated for us." I turned the page over. It was covered in Elven script, flowing and flourished. "It tells of an ancient temple deep in the Eastern Wastes, and the origin of the human Wild magic of shape-shifting."

Otsoa yowled and made a little hop away from the table. He had told me once that that was something he had been searching for himself before being pulled back to civilization on a different mission.

"We'll probably have to go to Rheste to find any more in-depth information about the legend," I added. After everything we had been through, I wanted to travel that far away from Cyfar.

"I can take care of the travel," Josie said, and set her fork down in a way that told me I couldn't argue the point. "And I know a place to stay there."

"I would come with you," Glenn said, then stopped as though not sure what to say next.

"You need to be here for Ura when she gets back," I finished for him. "I wouldn't expect anything different."

He smiled at me in thanks. "I'd be happier if you took another Warden with you, but I know that might not be possible."

I twisted my mouth in thought. "I might know a few people who would be discreet."

"I'd settle for a few people who know how to kill rabid animals." Glenn sighed. "Are you sure this is what you want to do?"

"It's what I have to do." I looked down at Otsoa, who was gazing at Josie. It was the least I could do. I pushed away the weight of guilt that threatened to drown me and looked around at the table at my family and friends. For now, at least, I was home, and I was going to enjoy every moment of it.

 * * *

More books from Melissa Matos

Warden's Cadence Series

Song of the Wild
Waltz of the Goblins
March of the Mad Mage (coming in 2022)

The Iron Sorcerer Series

available free at melissamatosauthor.com
The Iron Sorcerer
Captain of the Red Dawn
Wilder of the Dark Tide (coming 2022)